UNFINISHED BUSINESS

Buy

for Melodrama

Follow
Nisa Santiago

www.twitter.com/Nisa_Santiago

www.facebook.com/NisaSantiago

Order online at
bn.com, amazon.com, and
MelodramaPublishing.com

www.melodramapublishing.com

Library of Congress Control Number: 2015912273
ISBN-13: 978-1620780541
ISBN-10: 1620780542
First Edition: March 2016

Interior: Candace K. Cottrell
Cover Design: CandaceK. Cottrell
Cover Photo: Marion Designs
Cover Model: Vanessa
Editor: Brian Sandy

Printed in Canada

BOOKS BY NISA SANTIAGO

Unfinished Business

Nisa Santiago

ONE

Mack D rode silently in the backseat of his bulletproof Tahoe with Peaches next to him. Sophia and Eduardo Jr. were next to her in the seat, riding comfortably in the tricked-out SUV. Mack D talked to the kids with kindness, but Peaches was his main concern. She had an angelic smile, cute little face, and her innocence was charming. She held on to the balloon he'd given her. She was such a doll baby.

Mack D's right-hand man, Richard, guided the Tahoe across the Whitestone Bridge into the Bronx. They rolled up to the warehouse, where the guests were waiting, and the security gates opened for the Tahoe. As Richard drove inside, Mack D could see the twins from his seat. They were seated upright and badly beaten by his men, but they were still breathing, as instructed. He didn't want them dead. Not yet anyway.

All eyes were on the truck.

Apple and Kola, worried about the children, fixed their eyes in the direction of the Tahoe as the back door opened up. The sisters were pinned to the metal chairs, hunched over, and bleeding, their wrists restrained behind them. Swollen eye sockets, busted lips, cuts, and forming bruises camouflaged their beauty.

The men in the room fell silent as Mack D stepped out of the Tahoe, his presence carrying great weight in the room. When he showed up, he commanded everyone's attention. Dressed sharply in a black suit and wing-tip shoes, he strutted toward the sisters with a tiger's stride. His shoulders were broad, and his cold, menacing eyes remained transfixed on the twins. This man was notorious in the streets, from Washington, DC to New York. He lit a Cuban cigar and took a few pulls, savoring the flavor.

The kids climbed out of the Tahoe with Richard's help, and a slight look of relief showed in the twins' eyes. The children attempted to run over to the sisters, but Richard stopped them from approaching any closer.

Mack D looked at the twins for a moment.

When Apple had called him "Daddy," it struck a chord inside of him. He looked at her intensely and said, "You think I'm your daddy?"

Kola answered. "You don't recognize us?" She had to force the words out. Her ribs felt cracked, she was weak, and she felt lightheaded.

"Why should I?" Mack D was trying to recognize them. It was the only reason they were still alive. Apple uttering the word *Daddy* had placed his murderous intentions on hold.

His original plan was to murder the girlfriends of the young hoodlums, Jamel and Kamel. They had taken his son Damien's life, so he was going to take something from them. He'd tracked down Apple and Kola. He wanted to slaughter their families, make Jamel and Kamel suffer, and then torture and kill them both. He was that kind of cold.

Mack D was somewhat in denial that these two were his daughters. He had been with plenty of women since he was fifteen years old. He had sown his royal oats, and had placed his seed into many women and impregnated them—black, white, Asian, Hispanic. Over the years, he had allegedly fathered over thirty children, including three sets of twins, before his long stretch in an upstate prison.

There were a few ladies he'd fallen in love with, and a few kids he accepted as his own, like Damien. Damien was his pride and joy. He had Mack D's looks and traits, and was only nineteen when Jamel shot him down in the streets like a dog.

Rachel was Damien's mother, and she was one of Mack D's true loves back in the day. She was five nine and light-skinned with bright, twinkling eyes and long lashes, and her hair was a rich shade of mahogany. She was loyal. While he did a long bid, she took care of him and his son.

There were many kids whose paternity Mack D flat-out denied. The mothers wanted DNA tests and child support once they found out Mack D was making that drug money.

He didn't know Apple and Kola.

He had a pistol in his hand and placed it against Apple's forehead. His eyes said he wasn't bluffing.

Apple refused to show any fear. If it was her day to die, then so be it. "Not in front of my daughter!" she demanded.

The kids were standing a few feet away, watching in horror as Apple was about to be executed.

"Your lover boy took away my son," he said to Apple, cocking the trigger back. "Peaches, close your eyes, baby. Do as Momma says."

Kola frowned and barked, "You ready to kill your own family?"

"You're no kin of mines," he countered.

"We're Denise's daughters—Nichols' sisters. How can you not remember us?" Kola had to spew words out fast to save their lives.

The name Nichols definitely caught Mack D's attention. Of course, he remembered Denise and his daughter Nichols. How could he forget them? Nichols was raped and murdered and then dumped in the trash bin while he was away in prison. When Denise wrote Mack D and told him about what happened, the news broke his heart. Back then he didn't have an army of goons, triggermen, and a flourishing drug empire like he had today.

He'd wanted revenge for Nichols, but Supreme was killed before he got out. That didn't stop his wrath, though. Supreme had a momma, two little brothers, and a daughter. When Mack D was released from prison, he made them all permanently disappear. One by one, they were snatched up, tortured, murdered, and then buried on a plot of undeveloped land on Long Island, which the mob had used as a cemetery for decades.

Mack D didn't go on his murderous rampage because he had great love for Nichols; he hardly knew her. The revenge was for the simple fact that he felt violated. Someone had the audacity to take something that belonged to him.

Mack D removed the pistol from Apple's forehead. At the moment, she had redemption. It was a moment of relief.

"Denise is your mother?" he asked skeptically. Denise was another woman he'd fallen in love with. The things she did in the bedroom blew his mind.

"Yes," Apple and Kola said simultaneously.

Mack D continued to look closely at the twins. He was never father material, but he was around Apple and Kola until they were about ten years old. And they did call him Daddy.

In fact, they called lots of men daddy. Denise always had some man in her bed and around her kids. She was a whore, and it was a shock to everyone that she didn't have more kids by other men.

"Your mother, where is she now?" he asked the twins. He wanted to see his old flame.

"She's dead," Apple blurted out.

"Dead?" Mack D repeated, bewilderment in his tone. "How?"

"She was murdered years ago," Kola chimed. "After Nichols."

Mack D lingered on the news for a moment. Denise always lived a fast, hard life. He assumed her lifestyle finally caught up with her.

He stared at the twins deadpan. He felt grief, but it was brief, like the blinking of his eyes. Denise had meant something to him back in the days. She was once someone special in his life, but that was a long time ago.

"Yo, what you gonna do wit' these bitches?" one of his goons asked.

Mack D didn't rush to give his answer. He stood silent. One snap of his fingers could mean life or death for Apple and Kola.

"Untie them," he said all of a sudden.

One of his men replied with a confused look, "What?"

"I said fuckin' untie them," he said sternly.

"But Mack D, these bitches ain't kin to you. They don't share your blood. They fuckin' wit' your head. They the enemy and—"

Mack D pointed the gun at the man talking, quickly shutting him up. He was ready to take his life if he continued defying his orders.

"It's cool. You the boss."

Mack D's men wanted to see bloodshed. They wanted to avenge Damien's death. Though the sisters didn't pull the trigger themselves, they were part of the problem.

The twins were released from their restraints by Mack D's reluctant men. Apple was the first to be untied, and then Kola.

Richard approached Mack D to place his two cents into his friend's ear. He was truth to power. He whispered, "You forgetting about your son? He's dead because of their boyfriends. These bitches don't mean anything to you. Why let them go?"

"I have my reasons, Richard."

"I'm sure you do. But right now, your reasons don't look good in front of everyone," Richard replied coolly.

Mack D looked at Richard calmly. "The means will justify the end, my friend."

"I hope so." Having said his piece, Richard then stepped away from Mack D.

Apple and Kola stood up. They'd escaped death again. Their nine lives were counting down. The first thing they wanted to do was go over and hug the children tightly.

Apple asked, "Why let us go?"

"You been reprieved, and you ask questions?"

"There's a reason for everything," she countered. "And what about Jamel and Kamel?"

"For now, they live," he said. "And their debt is zeroed out. Y'all have no need to worry."

It was good news, but Apple and Kola remained suspicious of Mack D's motive.

Richard and his men thought Mack D had done lost his mind, but they didn't question him. The tension in the room was thick. It felt like everyone was breathing in stale air mixed with cyanide.

Finally, Apple and Kola were able to hug the children. It was a strong embrace filled with tears and emotions, like they had been separated from each other for years and it was a long-awaited reunion.

Mack D watched the happy reunion. Richard stood beside him, frowning. He fretted over Mack D's decision, but it wasn't his call. Damien was his friend. He wanted to see justice done.

"What now?" Apple asked, staring at Mack D.

"We keep in touch. This isn't over. We're not over. Do you both understand?"

The twins nodded.

"My son is dead because of y'all's lovers. But today I put my grief behind me. I know y'all wonder why. For the moment, just understand that today I'm your savior, and you don't have to worry about anything. You will be protected."

"Protected from what or who?" Apple asked.

Mack D chuckled lightly. He looked at Apple with coolness.

Kola gathered the children into her arms, while Apple kept her guard up. Mack D said they were free to go, but something just didn't feel right. He had to be plotting, and Apple didn't want to fall victim to something sinister. What bothered her most was he was allowing Kamel and Jamel to live, even though they'd killed his son. No one was that forgiving.

Mack D had them all blindfolded again and placed into the back of the van. They were leaving the same way they came, by the skin of their teeth. With the children riding with them, Apple and Kola were driven back to Coney Island.

Watching the van leave from the warehouse, Mack D turned to Richard, who was still standing next to him, and said, "Ignorance is a breeding ground for deception, my friend."

TWO

The rap music boomed throughout the Manhattan club, and the crowd inside danced as the loud beat bounced off the walls. The place was packed from wall to wall, the ladies were dressed in their sexiest outfits, and the liquor was flowing.

Jamel sat in the VIP area clutching a half-downed Moët bottle, nodding and singing along to Jay Z's and Kanye West's "Niggas in Paris" as it blared with the DJ's twist and mix. He was feeling the rhyme. He felt couldn't shit phase him. He was untouchable. No matter what, he was still going to do him and ball out hard. He refused to go into hiding and run away with his tail between his legs. He was a man. Bred to be a warrior.

He was going to continue to walk around with his chest out, despite a high contract out on his head and the deadly war he and his brother were fighting. He wanted to prove to everyone that he wasn't scared of anyone, especially Mack D. Though the man had a fierce reputation, at the end of the day, he was just a man, and he still could bleed like everyone else. Jamel was ready to prove that theory to the streets by spilling Mack D's brains out onto the concrete.

Jamel took a swig from the Moët and continued to nod to the upbeat song. Surrounded by friends, goons, and over five hundred clubgoers, what kept him protected was the pistol concealed in his ankle holster.

A chocolate brunette with big breasts, thick thighs, and a slim waist sat on his lap. Her bubbly personality was engaging, and her smile and laughter put him in a joyful mood. Her round ass massaged his crotch, and her flirtatious behavior indicated he was about to get lucky tonight.

With his hand deep between her thighs, he said into her ear, "Ma, you definitely shining bright like a diamond tonight."

She chuckled. "You so silly," she said.

"I'm many things, but silly ain't one," he said, offended. Jamel looked at the young, sexy beauty and quickly got over her innocent remark. "Listen, tonight's about having fun, right?"

"Yes, it is," she replied with an appealing smile.

When Rihanna's "Pour It Up" started to blast through the speakers, she jumped off his lap, dancing excitedly and singing along.

Jamel watched his newfound friend twerk and dance seductively in front of him, her short skirt rising up her thighs as she moved, flashing something lovely to him. He couldn't take his eyes off her. His dick grew hard just watching her.

"Yeah, it's definitely about to be a fun night." He took another mouthful of Moët, his eyes transfixed by her big booty and winding hips. He was yearning to reach out and touch her.

Apple and fidelity wasn't on his mind. He was in his environment and wanted to fuck some new pussy. She was just his type—thick, beautiful, and easy. He couldn't remember her name, but it didn't matter. In about an hour, he'd be ready to peel off her clothes.

Jamel took another mouthful of Moët, his eyes dancing up and down her body. He licked his lips and rubbed down his hard crotch, his intentions obvious. The only thing on his mind was pussy. Fuck his beef with Mack D! Tonight, it was about him, and he was ready to thrust himself into lust and absolute partying. Forget about tomorrow; it was about right now.

Outside the club, a silver four-door Lexus came to a stop, parking against regulations on the street. The driver had more important matters to worry about than getting a ticket or his car being towed. The door opened, and Kamel stepped out onto the pavement.

The line to get inside wrapped around the corner, and security outside the club was sharp and tight, all brawny and clad in black muscle shirts.

Kamel marched ahead, ignoring the long line, his 9 mm concealed in a holster underneath his jacket. His expression deadpan, he was determined to enter the popular club with his piece. Without it, he felt like a dead man walking, vulnerable to the wolves that were plotting his demise. He had enemies lurking everywhere, and most likely watching his every move.

Kamel wasn't concerned about the bouncers standing outside. They weren't a problem for him. He stepped toward security guarding the entrance like he was a tidal wave approaching. They immediately recognized his face and stepped aside, allowing him entry without a search. He walked inside like he owned the place. Kamel was friends with the owners of Club Cream, and it was well known to the club employees that Maxwell and Hendrix were involved with the twins in many endeavors, from moving drugs through the club to money laundering.

Kamel was the brains; Jamel was the crazy one—the killer.

Kamel hastily navigated his way through the thick crowd, urgently approaching the VIP area, where he knew Jamel would be. The place was dim with strobe lights flashing, music blaring, and pretty young ladies everywhere, but none of it caught his attention. He had only one purpose—finding his twin brother.

Kamel walked into the VIP area and quickly found Jamel socializing with the usual groupie bitches and drinking liquor. He approached his brother with a rigid frown and smacked the bottle out of his hands, shouting, "Are you fuckin' stupid? Did you fuckin' forget?"

His actions startled everyone around. People looked on at the identical twins, but no one said a word.

Jamel stood up, angry that Kamel smacked the bottle from his hands and humiliated him in front of everyone. "Nigga, you fuckin' crazy!"

"We at war, and you out here frolicking like everything is all good, like we got peace out there. I told you, keep a low profile."

Jamel, his face twisted in anger, stepped closer to his brother. He was up in his face. "Fuck a low profile! You think I give a fuck about niggas out here tryin' to get at me? I buss my fuckin' gun too!"

Kamel tried to keep his composure. Jamel was always the stupid, out of control, shoot-first-and-not-think-of-the-consequences type of nigga. He could end up getting them both killed.

"I'm trying to protect you," Kamel said.

"Nigga, I don't need any fuckin' protection," Jamel quickly countered. "You should know I'm able to handle myself."

"You need to think, muthafucka! Think!"

The crowd in VIP watched as the twins created a scene. Most were already aware of the war between them and Mack D. The ladies were enthralled by the bad boys.

The fellows surrounding Jamel were down for whatever. In their world, it was either kill or be killed. Jamel and Kamel were their gravy train, so they were willing to protect their bosses at any cost.

"Yo, nigga, walk away and let me be," Jamel growled. "I got this under control."

Kamel didn't want to continue to cause a scene in a place where they did business. He glared at his twin for a moment. He wanted to punch Jamel in the face and drag him out of there; knock some sense into him.

"Now, before I was interrupted by this foolishness, I was having a really good time not thinking about this bullshit," Jamel said sharply. "Fuck I look like to you?"

Jamel picked up another fresh bottle of champagne from the table nearby, popped it open, and took a lengthy guzzle right in front of Kamel. Then he signaled for the pretty chocolate groupie that had been keeping him company to come over.

And she did.

Jamel took a seat imposingly in front of Kamel and pulled the girl by her forearm down on his lap, groping her openly for everyone to see. They both had no shame in their game. He looked up at his brother and said, "You gonna continue to intrude on my good time, muthafucka? I don't know about you, but I'm tryin' to fuck tonight. You need to take ya gay ass out the fuckin' door and let a nigga be."

Kamel's ringing cell phone distracted his attention from Jamel. It was Kola.

"You stupid!" he said to Jamel right before taking Kola's call. He pivoted from Jamel's direction and walked away.

Everything behind him was returning back to normal. Jamel and his cronies continued taking delight in pussy and champagne.

"Hey, baby. Everything okay?" Kamel said into the phone.

"Kamel, I need to see you," Kola cried.

Kamel instantly knew something was wrong by the sound of her voice. He was no longer concerned about Jamel. He hurried away from his brother.

"Baby, what's wrong? Where are you?" The phone was glued to his ear, as he tried to drown out the noise from the club.

"We were just with him."

"You were with who?"

"Mack D! He took us hostage."

"What!"

The name made Kamel so angry, the hair on his arms stood up. He immediately thought the worst. All kinds of cruel thoughts started to swim around in his head. He hurried outside, trying to extract as much information from her as possible.

Once outside the club, he asked, "Baby, where are you now?"

"I'm at your place," she announced.

He was relieved somewhat. "Are you alone?"

"Just hurry here."

"I'm already there," he said.

Was it a setup? Was Mack D on the other end listening, plotting to kill him once he walked into the apartment? How did Mack D find Kola? How was he going to handle it?

Kamel jumped into his Lexus, which was untouched—no parking tickets, no issue—started the ignition, and sped away. He removed his pistol and prepared himself for anything coming his way.

THREE

Kamel climbed the stairway to his apartment. He gripped his pistol, a round already in the chamber, as he moved to the apartment door with caution. Was death waiting for him on the other side of the door? He called Kola from his cell phone again.

"I'm outside," he said. "Open the door, if you can."

Soon after, the door opened, and Kola loomed into his view. One look at her and Kamel was devastated.

"What the fuck!"

Kola's battered and beaten face screamed out at him like a banshee.

"Baby, what happened to you?" Kamel walked inside with his eyes tearing up.

Kola looked like she'd gotten into the ring with an angry Mike Tyson and gone a full twelve rounds with him. Kamel was furious.

"Who did this to you? Mack D? I'm gonna kill that muthafucka!" he said through clenched teeth.

Kola hated that he had to see her like this, but she couldn't hide the way she looked from him.

Kamel followed her into the living room, thirsting for information. The apartment was quiet, but his heart was thumping with a need to seek revenge.

"Where are the kids?" he asked.

"They're sleeping."

"Where's Apple? Is she coming here too?"

Kola shrugged. "I left her a spare key, but she's not answering my calls."

"What happened?"

"We need to talk," she said.

She sat on the couch, and he sat next to her with a serious and concerned look. He didn't want to think about what Mack D might have done to his woman. The tears trickling down his face was proof enough of how much he loved her.

"It's a long story."

"I'm listening, baby," he said coolly.

She looked at Kamel, locking eyes with his dark pupils. She could see the anger. "He's my father."

"He's your what?" he exclaimed, his eyes wide open. This was news way out of the ballpark.

"He's not my biological father, but he was my little sister's father, Nichols. Remember? I told you about her."

Kamel nodded.

"My mother was in love with him, but I remembered him as a two-bit hustler, not the kingpin he is now. And we called him Daddy, or by his real name, Domencio. We didn't know this new Mack D persona he has. I haven't seen him since I was ten. He was in and out of jail."

Kamel was dumbfounded by what he was hearing. He couldn't believe Mack D had the audacity to hurt his own step-daughter. How grimy could the man be? But there was no excuse why Kola's face was beaten to shit.

"What did he say to you? Why did he let you go?"

"He released us with no just cause; just set me and my sister free."

"No reason at all? No conditions, retribution, or anything?"

She shook her head. "No."

Kamel rubbed his chin for a moment. "What about Jamel and me?"

"He said we are all protected, that the debt is zeroed out, and that he had put all his grief behind him."

Kamel's face showed a blended look of confusion and anger. "It don't make fuckin' sense. What the fuck is he talkin' about? Is he joking?"

"I don't know what's going on, baby. I wish I could explain it better."

"Why'd he beat on you like this? What else did he say or do, Kola? What else!"

He didn't mean to snap at her, but he was nervous and didn't understand what was going on. There were too many questions and no answers at all.

Kamel was grateful that Apple and Kola were alive. Mack D was known to be ruthless to men *and* women. They should have been dead. Why did he let them go? Was it because he had known the twins since they were young, fucked their mother, and they were kin to his biological daughter? And what did he mean by they were "protected?"

"We need to think and be very careful from now on, baby. All this, it doesn't make any sense."

"It doesn't," Kola agreed.

Kamel didn't know what to do or how to react. He was ready to take Mack D's head off and kick it into the river.

He pulled Kola into his arms, holding her close. Guilt trickled inside of him because this wasn't her beef. It wasn't even Apple's. Jamel started this. Kamel backed his brother, but not at the expense of Kola's life. He should have been there for her. He wasn't there to protect her, like he'd promised. It bothered him.

He soothed Kola, rubbing her shoulders, kissing her wounds, touching her hair, promising her that everything was going to be okay. Whatever sinister plan Mack D had brewing, it wasn't going to harm them. Kamel planned to be ready. It was about to be a fight to the very end.

Apple had Kola worried. He didn't care where her twin sister went. She was unpredictable, like Jamel. They were the same. His main concern was Kola and the children.

Kamel picked up Kola into his arms, being gentle with her bruised body, and carried her into the bedroom. He closed the door and undressed her slowly. He kissed her again, nursed her wounds, and then said she needed her rest and placed her under the covers. He stayed with her until she drifted off to sleep.

Then he stood up and walked out of the Brooklyn apartment. He went up to the rooftop and gazed out at the city. The fresh air was welcoming. He stood on the gravel and lit a cigarette, the 9 mm tucked in his waistband. He never left home without it.

No matter how beautiful the night was, Kamel couldn't take his mind off the threatening situation with his girl and Mack D. She had been too close to death. Things needed to change. He felt they needed to move differently—be more careful. They had been caught slipping. The enemy had gotten too close, and not only were the sisters in harm's way, but so were the children.

Kamel took a pull from the burning Newport between his lips and inhaled the cigarette smoke. He continued gazing at the city from the top of his building, a full moon above. He needed to do something. He didn't want to sit around and wait for something to happen.

Mack D had made his move, but it didn't make any sense. The more Kamel thought about it, the more puzzling it was to him. There was no way a man like Mack D could be that forgiving over the murder of his son. It seemed like groundwork for some malicious plan to be implemented.

Kamel finished off his cigarette and flicked it off the rooftop. He stood there in the breezy night, still like a statue, his mind contemplating. He needed to direct his own pawns and make his move. His first and only priority was to protect his queen by any means necessary.

He stepped closer to the ledge and peered over. The streets below were busy with traffic and people. It felt good to see the neighborhood from a bird's-eye view. If only he had a view like this over what his foes were plotting—see the problems coming from afar. He would be like a sniper, perched above with his high-powered rifle and, one by one, he could pick off the enemies as they came his way. Nothing but head shots.

Kamel pulled out his cell phone and made a call.

The phone rang several times, and then Timothy answered, "Long time."

"It has been, but I didn't call to catch up on lost time."

"What's going on? You okay?" Timothy asked.

"I need a favor."

"You know favors cost."

"I know. I wouldn't have called if I wasn't ready to pay."

"I'm listening."

"Not over the phone," Kamel said. "Meet me tomorrow evening in Prospect Park."

"I'm there."

Kamel ended the call. He was preparing for the worst.

FOUR

t was three in the morning when Jamel decided to leave the club and continue his fun elsewhere. For him, the night was still young. The liquor had him tipsy, but he was still focused. His dick was hard, and he was ready to fuck or have his dick sucked. He walked out the club with his beauty on his arm.

He fondled her butt and cupped her tit. "Damn, ma, ya body is tight."

"Thank you, baby," she said, encouraging him. She was easy with a capital *E*.

Jamel walked to his Benz parked across the street. He stumbled a little but didn't fall. The alcohol didn't take him completely.

His prized bimbo, looking like the perfect trophy piece, became his support. Her beauty, long legs, tight dress, and long hair caught niggas' attention outside. She strutted with Jamel, her high heels working the pavement.

Before they could get to his Benz, Jamel's hands were all over her. They stopped in the middle of the street, and he shoved his tongue down her throat. His hands reached down and cupped her round ass cheeks. He was putting on a show for those outside watching. He was tempted to lift her dress up to her hips and expose her ass to the men watching and hating.

After their passionate kiss, they continued toward the car, laughing and being touchy-feely with each other.

They climbed into the Benz, and Jamel adjusted the pistol in his ankle holster. Then he removed the Glock 17 from underneath the driver's seat and put it in the glove compartment. He didn't hide who he was. He was a gangsta twenty-four/seven. He loved the street life, the drugs, the women, and the murder. He loved having a reputation as a dangerous man.

"Guns don't scare you, right?" he said.

"The bigger the gun, the better the recoil," she said, smiling at him.

He grabbed his crotch. "I'm gonna give you a gun to play with tonight."

She continued smiling and placed her hand on his thigh. They looked at each other, their sexual tension building. It was clear that they wanted to fuck each other's brains out.

Jamel placed his hand on her open, smooth thigh and moved his touch upward. He licked his lips. The heat between her thighs was alluring.

He started the car but didn't put the it into DRIVE yet. He was in no rush to leave. Not with this young beauty sexually attacking him with her sweet touch and tender kisses, and the liquor coaxing his lustful appetite.

Her lips moved swiftly from his ear to his neck, and the touch of her hot breath on his skin shot through his mind in burning lines. The girl bit just above his collarbone and then higher to his jaw. She sucked at him as if she was drinking from him.

His right hand seemed to move of its own volition, slowly, as he started at the absolute perfection of the girl's full breasts. He pushed the material of her dress aside, exposing her small, dark nipple. He cupped her breast, feeling the nipple in the center of his palm, and then took it into his mouth.

The girl moaned, and her hand went to his crotch. She stroked and grabbed at him through his pants. She pulled at his belt and was able to unbuckle it effortlessly. She undid his pants and exposed his erection. Her manicured hand stroked him gently.

"Suck my dick," he said.

She simply folded herself into his lap, her hand still gripping his hard flesh, and took the dick into her mouth.

"Damn, ma, I'm lovin' you already."

As her head bobbed up and down, entertaining his dick with her wet, full lips, his cell phone rang.

He picked up his phone and saw that it was Apple calling. He had no intention of answering.

As the girl continued sucking his dick, he moaned and grabbed the back of her head, her long hair entangled in his fingers.

His cell phone rang again, and he ignored it.

While she orally pleasured him, Jamel put the car in drive and left the block. There was too much activity going on around him. Clubgoers were leaving the club, traffic was becoming thick, and police was starting to come around.

With the car moving, the girl didn't stop her action. She focused on him, while he focused on the road.

Several blocks from the club, Jamel's hard dick was still being absorbed into her mouth. She was a beast.

Jamel peered through his rearview mirror and noticed a car following him closely. He swore it'd been behind him since he'd left the club. He was paranoid. While stopped at a red light, he reached over the girl deep-throating him and massaging his balls, and opened the glove compartment to retrieve his gun.

He drove two blocks and stopped at another red light. While idling at the intersection, he said to the girl, "Hold up for a second, ma. I need to handle something real quick."

She rose up, her tits out, thong showing, and wiping pre-cum from her mouth. She knew something was going on, seeing the Glock in his hand and the coldness in his eyes. She remained cool. "What's going on?"

He quickly fastened his jeans. "Duck down," he told her.

The minute she hunkered down in the passenger seat, Jamel slid out from the driver's seat, the gun in his hand, his arm outstretched toward the vehicle behind him, and he quickly opened up. The explosion from the Glock was ear-shattering.

Bak! Bak! Bak! Bak!Bak! Bak! Bak!

Bullets went flying at the car, shattering the windshield. The occupants in the front seats ducked for cover.

"Y'all coming for me, huh? Fuck wit' me!" he shouted. "You know who the fuck I am?" He continued firing, riddling the car with bullets, not caring who was nearby witnessing.

Satisfied that he had proven his point, he hopped back into his car and sped away, leaving everyone around bewildered and shocked.

Jamel blew through two red lights, the smoking gun on his lap.

The girl sat silent and wide-eyed.

Jamel looked at her and managed to smile. "Yo, sorry about that, ma. Gotta let these niggas know who they fuckin' wit'. A nigga got a contract on his life. Anyway, you gonna finish what you started?" He unzipped his pants and pulled out his hard cock.

She hesitated, but Jamel wasn't taking no for an answer.

He looked her way. "What the fuck you waiting for? Finish suckin' my dick. That shit was feelin' good, ma."

She leaned over into his lap and slowly engulfed his erect penis.

His dick throbbed inside her mouth, the car racing through the street. "I like you, ma. You definitely gangsta."

She closed her eyes and continued pleasing him.

Jamel parked the car somewhere secluded. He pushed against her, his gun close to his reach, already cocked back and ready.

She took hold of Jamel's condom-protected dick and straddled him, guiding him into her.

Sliding into her seemed like the purest sensation of his life, or in a very long time. He was enveloped, buried in her unnatural heat, searing impossibly hot against him, and she gyrated her hips, feeling the hard dick cemented inside of her.

"Ooooh yeah, give me that good pussy. Feels so good. Oh fuck!" he grunted, his hands against her phat ass.

He closed his eyes, every part of him in pure bliss. She held his wrists and arched her back as they fucked. He opened his eyes and saw that she was watching him, her mouth open, her eyes half closed. His dick made her forget about the shooting.

Jamel's cell phone rang for the umpteenth time that night. It was Apple calling. Once again, he ignored it.

She rode him faster, her fingers gripping his wrists to the point where it was beginning to hurt. The windows fogged up from their lust inside the car, the heat from their breaths and bodies lingering like a strong smell.

She began to moan, and he began to moan even louder. She pressed her body against his, thrashing on top of him, her breath rasping. He reclined back in his seat as waves of shockingly bright pleasure rocked his body with every movement. The pussy was good.

Her hips bucking wildly, her breath on his face, he could feel every millimeter inside her—slick, muscular, and feverishly hot.

She threw her head back, yelping from the back of her throat, and he could feel his own orgasm cresting.

When he came, it felt like a gun going off.

They both shuddered in the driver's seat, her legs clamped tightly around him, as she was rocked with a strong orgasm. She screamed against his neck, and he felt his own cry echoing hers involuntarily.

Relaxed and satisfied, he said loudly, "I love this shit!"

FIVE

Apple stared at her bruises and swollen eye in the bathroom mirror. She looked horrible. The look of her broken face angered her so much she screamed. She clenched her fist and rammed it into the mirror, spider-webbing the glass. She wanted to cut off Mack D's genitals and shove them in his mouth. How dare he have his goons put their hands on her? Mack D had made the mistake of letting her go. She planned on running into him again, and this time, the odds would be in her favor. The only thing on Apple's mind was violence and gunplay. Fuck his protection! She was ready to start hunting down his men and do what she did best.

She tended to her wounds the best she could. Her right eye was swollen shut, and her lip was busted. Her loaded pistol rested on the sink counter, next to the peroxide and bandages. The fire in her eyes wasn't about to burn out anytime soon.

Apple was skeptical about everything Mack D had said to them. She didn't trust him at all. The fact that he wasn't their biological father, didn't really raise them, nor took care of his own daughter Nichols told her that she should continue watching her back.

Apple finished tending to her bruises and exited the bathroom. She picked up her cell phone and tried to continually reach Jamel. No answer. His cell phone went straight to voice mail. She wondered where he was and why he wasn't picking up. She wanted to see him. She needed his masculine touch and reassurance.

It was becoming lonely in the Manhattan apartment she shared with Kola, who'd decided to take the children and stay at Kamel's place in Brooklyn. Kamel and Kola's relationship was almost perfect. Kamel would do anything for her sister. He was always there, loving her wholeheartedly.

Jamel was such the opposite. He was impulsive and half-assed with their relationship, most times.

Where is he? Apple knew he was in the club, partying heavily and trying to fuck the next bitch. She didn't trust him, but she needed him. She wanted to love him, but Jamel was a hard man to love. Most times, he was selfish and a complete moron. He was undependable, ignoring her phone calls in an emergency.

She walked into the empty living room and looked around. Though it could get lonely, the solitude was what she needed. She needed time to think. What would be her next move?

Sighing heavily, she took a seat on the couch and expertly rolled up two blunts of Kush and got lifted. She needed to temporarily escape her troubles. Apple sat back, relaxed, and let the high take over.

Apple climbed out of the car beneath a sunny, blue sky. The weather was temperate, and the area she was in was comforting, with sprawling cut grass, sparse traffic, and seclusion.

She walked alone into the cemetery carrying a bouquet of white roses. She took a deep breath. She was dressed in all black, her long black hair styled into a ponytail. She traveled deeper into the cemetery, searching for her sister's grave. It'd been a long time since she'd paid her respects. The guilt was still seeded inside of her, entangled around her core, like large vines. She could never forget.

This was always difficult—coming to her little sister's gravesite and cruelly being reminded how she was killed. The sight of Nichols' name on the tombstone brought her to tears.

"I'm so sorry," she said in a broken voice. "I am, baby sister. I should be the one lying there, not you."

She dropped to her knees and placed the bouquet of flowers onto the grave. Then she lowered her head, closed her eyes, and filled her mind with memories of Nichols, reminiscing on the life she lived.

Nichols was a sweet and smart girl who'd fallen victim to the evil of the streets. She had a future. She had dreams. It wasn't Nichols' fault. The devil came after Nichols instead of her—the true perpetrator.

It would always be Apple's perpetual nightmare. The night terror she was never going to wake up from. It was her choice to get involved with Supreme. Going to the Summer Jam concert in style was more important than anything else. She'd borrowed from a demon. When he came to collect, instead of paying him, she tried to run and hide, and then belittle him. The end result was her innocent little sister buried in the cold ground.

Apple rose to her feet, her eyes still fixated on the tombstone. "I miss you so much, Nichols," she stated, tears trickling from her eyes. "You know, so much has changed. I have a daughter now, and she is my everything. Her name is Peaches. You would love her, Nichols. She is adorable. You would have been such a great aunt to your niece. I know you would."

Apple stood silent. Her memories were taking her away to another place. She thought about Nichols' beauty and her character, and then that tragic day. It would be something she would never forget. A hundred years could go by, and her feelings of guilt would never change.

"I've been through so much, little sister. You couldn't even imagine. Every day I'm haunted by what happened to you, and every day I wish I could change it. I'd take your place in a heartbeat. If you were here instead of me, then this world would probably be a much better place.

"I set fire to a lot of things and became poison to everything around me. When you died, I died. Then I made everyone else die.

"I became a killer—Can you believe that? I know you don't want to hear that about me, but I came to tell you the truth. You deserve the truth. You was always upbeat and positive, Nichols, no matter what happened to you. And the monsters that did this to you, I made them burn in hell."

Apple fell silent again, flooded with more memories, more pain. She took a deep breath.

"I'm sorry I haven't been coming to visit you lately, that I stayed away from you for so long, but this is hard for me, Nichols. It is. I kept away because I knew I was responsible for this. Please forgive me." She stepped closer to the tombstone and placed her hands against it. She crouched slightly, wrapping her arms around it, embracing the hard granite like Nichols was in her arms.

She closed her eyes again, feeling close to her sister. She felt a cool breeze against her skin and the sun in her face. It was soothing. It felt like her sister had put her hands on her, embracing her back.

"I love you, Nichols. I promise I won't stay away so long. Next time, I'll bring Peaches." Apple pivoted and walked back to her car. Her heart felt like it was in her stomach, like it was sinking in quicksand. She felt sick and sad, her mood crashing.

Apple climbed into her car and lingered behind the steering wheel for a moment, looking distant. Drying away the tears, she took a deep breath and started the ignition. She gave one final look at the cemetery and said, "I'll be back."

While driving, she tried dialing Jamel again. She didn't get an answer. Like a dozen times before, her call went straight to his voice mail.

Stupid muthafucka!

It'd been over twenty-four hours since her run-in with Mack D, and she needed to talk to him.

She drove to Kamel's apartment in Brooklyn, where she knew her sister would be with the kids. Kola felt safe there.

Apple refused to go into hiding, knowing Kamel would suggest it to her sister. Mack D probably was watching them. It was all probably a setup. She didn't want to run from her battle, and she'd didn't expect Kola to run either. Where they came from, they always stood their ground, no matter what.

She parked in front of Kamel's Williamsburg apartment and got out. She hurried into the building and took the stairs. When she walked inside, no one was home. The place was empty—no children, no Kola, and no Kamel.

She called Kola's cell phone immediately. She picked up.

"Where are you?" Apple asked.

"With Kamel. We left. He felt it wasn't safe for us there anymore."

"Where is he taking y'all?"

"We don't know yet. But it's somewhere no one will know us. We want you to meet us."

"You know I don't run, Kola. Mack D don't put fear in my heart."

"It's not about fear, it's about being smart. It's about surviving for your daughter. You need to think about her, Apple. For once, you need to start thinking about your family."

"I always think about her. And when the world is safe around her, then I can relax. I lost her once. I will not lose her again."

"Apple, I love you. We all love you."

"I love y'all too."

"Don't go out there and do anything stupid."

"Come on now, Kola. Don't insult me. I ain't new to this shit."

"You just need to come with us and lay low. We can think of a plan."

"You have your plan, and I have mines," Apple replied. "Just continue keeping my daughter safe." She hung up.

Apple walked around the apartment. Without the kids' laughter and the warmth of family around, it was just another cold place. Cold like her life had been for years. She didn't want to be alone and away from her family, especially not after finally getting her daughter back. But there was a situation that needed to be handled.

Peaches was the most important thing to her in the world, and she was going to do everything in her power to protect her.

Thirsty and hungry, Apple walked into the kitchen and opened the refrigerator. As she looked inside, ready to reach for a bottle of juice and a sandwich, she heard the front door to the apartment open.

Cautious, she picked up her gun and went toward the door slowly. Whoever made the mistake of breaking into the apartment was about to learn the hard way that they'd made a bad choice.

She quickly emerged from around the corner and aimed center mass at the intruder. The barrel suddenly was in someone's face. She glared at him, and before her trigger finger got itchy, she realized it was Jamel.

Jamel saw the gun in Apple's hand, and he didn't even flinch. "Damn! This the warm welcoming a nigga comes home to?"

"Where the fuck was you? I tried calling you all night."

"I was out taking care of business."

He reeked of pussy and booze. His eyes looked tired, his lips were chapped, and his clothes were disheveled. It looked like he hadn't slept or showered in days.

"What the fuck happened to ya face?" he asked, finally noticing her bruises.

"Mack D is what happened to my face."

"What the fuck are you talking about?"

Apple frowned as she lowered the gun. His infidelity was becoming wearisome, and his lack of concern for their relationship was growing out of control. But she kept her cool.

"My sister and me had a serious run-in with Mack D," she said "He kidnapped us and the children."

"He did what? He put his fuckin' hands on you?" Jamel asked, sounding like a concerned boyfriend now.

He stepped closer to Apple. His actions last night were in the past. Now, he wanted to pull her into his arms and show his love. Become her bodyguard, like Kevin Costner to Whitney Houston. The sight of her face aggravated him.

"Yo, I'ma kill that muthafucka!"

"Where were you when I needed you? I've been calling and calling."

"I was out there taking care of business, like I told you before."

Apple wasn't a fool. She knew what kind of business he was taking care of. It was clearly written all over him. The smell on his clothes, her unanswered phone calls. Jamel was never the subtle type. Apple would have to deal with that another time. She had more important things to take care of.

He tried to touch the side of her face, but she rejected his caress. She didn't want it. She frowned. She hated him at that moment. She hated feeling weak and vulnerable for him.

"How did he get at you?" Jamel asked.

The question was irrelevant. She was still alive. Now the more important question was, how could she get at him?

"There's more to tell you," she said.

"Like what?"

The smell of him continued to sicken her. Her disgust had to be put on the backburner. She said, "Mack D is my father."

"He's your what?"

"Not biological," she said quickly. "He's my stepfather, or he was once."

"Get the fuck outta here! I need to hear this shit!" Jamel was ready to pull up a chair and listen intently to what Apple had to say. Like a child sitting around a campfire, he was ready for the ghost stories.

Apple went on to explain the situation to him, which she found somewhat difficult. Apple couldn't believe it herself.

Jamel couldn't believe his ears. And when she said he was reprieved, he was befuddled.

"What you mean, reprieved? He tryin' to let that shit go?"

"I don't know what he's tryin' to do. But he says he wants to forget about it. He sayin' you and Kamel's debts are paid off."

"I know this nigga ain't that stupid, baby. He done lost his fuckin' mind! But you know what this means; we can get in close to him—sit down and talk. I mean, if he's that stupid to kidnap you and Kola and let y'all go, talking about some reprieve shit, especially when I murked his son, then that nigga is a stupid muthafucka, and he needs to be got. He ain't right upstairs."

"I don't want anything to do with politicking with him," Apple said. "I want that muthafucka dead!"

"This is our time, baby! Our time! You feel me?"

Apple wasn't feeling Jamel at all. But she was willing to at least try to.

SIX

It was late afternoon when Kamel parked his Denali near Ocean Avenue and looked around Prospect Park. Prospect Park was not as dramatic as Central Park. It was an urban park with room to explore and play, with multiple trails circumnavigating as well as slicing through the landscape. A few joggers and cyclists stuck to the paved roadways, while dog walkers, a few school kids, and ramblers meandered toward the core. There was a huge open meadow near the middle, several historic structures, a grand arch like in Paris, places to picnic and play sports, a zoo, and a botanical garden across the street.

But Kamel wasn't there for what the park had to offer. It would be a great place to bring the kids, but it would have to wait until after they were safe. He was there only for business. It was the designated spot to meet Timothy.

The parking lot he sat in was sparse with cars. He lit a cigarette and remained patient. He couldn't stop thinking about the threat to him and his family. Kamel would give his life for the woman he loved. He was scared, more so for Kola and the kids. A man like Mack D could come at him in so many different ways, not just in the streets. Mack D was connected politically and was rumored to be a Five Percenter.

While he waited, Kamel kept his .45 near his reach. Although he trusted Timothy, he wasn't about to take any chances with his life. There was no telling how extensive Mack D's influence was. He could corrupt anyone easily for the right price.

Thinking about Kola and the kids put a smile on Kamel's face. They'd put something special back into his life. He loved being around them. If he was away from them for even a minute, he started to miss them.

Though Kamel was a thug with a violent resume, he had dreams and goals he wanted to accomplish. Kamel was nothing like his twin brother Jamel, who was a psychopath with no direction, no heart, and no compassion. He didn't have long-term goals and was too spontaneous. Jamel lived his life day by day, high off the thrill of going over 100mph in the dark, hands off the steering wheel on an icy, winding road. It was inevitable that he would crash soon.

Headlights approached the parking lot. Kamel kept his eyes on the burgundy Lexus with expensive rims approaching. It was definitely Timothy showing up.

Kamel perked up. He grabbed his pistol, stuffed it into his waistband, and covered it with his T-shirt. "Here we go," he said.

Timothy parked opposite of him. Kamel could see only one silhouette through the windshield.

He climbed out his truck and coolly walked toward the Lexus.

Timothy and Kamel went back ten years. Timothy was a former US Marine and had done one tour overseas in war-torn Afghanistan. His military training gave him knowledge about guns and how to snuff out someone. He had also served time in prison. He and Kamel were once cellmates in Sing Sing and became good friends after Kamel saved his life while inside.

One cold evening in the yard, two men approached Timothy, one gripping a sharp shank. Kamel stood in the distance and picked up on the danger. Before the men could make a move on his friend, Kamel slammed himself into the man with the shank and forced him to the ground. He was all over him with his fists, punching him wildly. Timothy took care of the friend, knocking the man out with two punches. Before the guards could break it up, Kamel and Timothy had viciously beaten both men. The fight got them ninety days in solitary. Timothy felt indebted to Kamel for having his back. Whenever Kamel had a problem, he was there to help take care of it.

Now, Timothy was the sergeant-at-arms of a street gang called "The Blood of Sons." He was an enforcer for his gang and was often used to carry out killings.

Tonight, Kamel didn't need him to carry out a hit. Timothy was expensive, and Kamel had used up all his favors with his friend. They rarely kept in contact, but when he needed him, Kamel always knew the number he needed to call to reach him.

Timothy was an attractive man, a mix of black and Latino. He had light caramel brown skin, with dark eyes and curly black hair, and he was tall and lean.

Kamel got into the passenger side of the Lexus. He gave Timothy dap and said, "How you been?"

"I'm good, my dude. It's been a long time."

"I know. Too long."

Timothy, never one for small talk, said, "What you call me out here for?"

"I need guns and a small favor."

"What kind of guns? You in trouble? And how small is the favor?"

"I can pay you for some guns, and the favor—you still own that house in Staten Island?"

"Yeah, it's vacant. It needs a little upkeep, though."

"It'll be perfect."

"A'ight, it's yours for five hundred a month."

"I got you. And the heat?"

"What kind of trouble you into? This kind of trouble?" Timothy pulled up his shirt and showed the 9 mm tucked in his waistband, "Or you need me to pop the trunk, let you flip through the catalog?"

"I need you to pop the trunk."

"You at war, my nigga?"

"I'm just being cautious."

"Ain't nothing wrong with being cautious. C'mon, let's do business. I got a hot African bitch waiting for me to work that pussy."

Kamel laughed.

Timothy climbed out of the car and walked around to the trunk, with Kamel right behind him. Timothy looked around the parking lot, making sure everything was clear, and there wasn't any unwanted attention. They were in the cut, anyway, away from the main street and from Brooklyn traffic.

Timothy opened the trunk, revealing the contents inside—enough powerful guns and assault rifles to supply a small army.

"Damn!"

"You like the package?"

"I see you still have your military connect."

"I gotta make this money and support my bitches."

"I see."

"What you looking to spend?"

"About ten stacks."

"A'ight, decent enough."

Kamel had his eyes on an IMI Uzi and a MGC Car-15 rifle. Both weapons could slice a man in half. "I like the selection."

"Kamel, you know I always come with the best toys."

"I know, and I do like my toys. The Uzis—how much for four of those?"

"You, my nigga, eight hundred a piece; they usually go for a stack."

"A'ight, I'll take those, and six of those Desert Eagles."

"You got good taste."

Kamel handed Timothy a brown paper bag with ten thousand dollars in cash inside. Timothy placed his friend's selection into a large duffel bag and handed the duffel to him.

After the transaction, Kamel got back into his Denali and drove out the parking lot, his bag full of guns on the backseat. He felt secure for now. Next, it was back to the hotel in New Jersey, where Kola and the kids were staying temporarily.

SEVEN

Mack D lit his Cuban cigar, took a long puff, and exhaled. He sat in his home office, reclined in a high-back leather chair behind his large desk. The muted flat-screen mounted on the wall opposite him showed the latest Dow Jones Industrial Average report. He glanced repeatedly at the numbers going across the bottom of the TV screen.

For many, the numbers on the TV read like hieroglyphics, but to Mack D, it was easy to decipher. He'd learned about the stock market while in prison. His cellmate was Charlie, an ex-broker who was doing twenty years for murdering his wife.

Charlie was a wiz when it came to investing money. He'd been a broker at Fidelity, one of the top-five firms.

Charlie and Mack D became friends. Charlie taught Mack D everything there was to know about investing and the stock market. They visited the prison library together on a daily basis. The books kept Mack D busy. He loved learning about money and how to make more of it.

Once Mack D got out, he put his newfound knowledge to use. Not only did he jump head-first back into the drug game, but he dove nose-first into investing, buying stocks, and building a business portfolio for himself. He became a dominant figure in business and in the streets. He invested in stocks, real estate, and operated a few cash-and-carry businesses in the city. Mack D cemented his influence with a few political leaders, cops, and judges, while becoming one of the largest drug kingpins in the city.

Mack D leaned back in his high-back leather chair and busied himself with his laptop for a moment. The marketwatch.com website gathered his attention. His office was quiet and decorated with leather couches and armchairs and expensive artwork. A collection of hardcover books sat on the three shelves against his wall, including Robert Greene's *The 48 Laws of Power* and *The Art of Seduction*. He had gone from being a two bit hoodlum to a rich, well respected, suit-and-tie-wearing muthafucka. He had definitely come a long way.

Mack D also became a Five Percenter convert in prison. They accepted him though he wasn't 100% black. He studied hard, learning their ways and beliefs. He was educated that he was a God.

Mack D loved the respect they got from the other inmates, and how the religion taught its people their true history. It was knowledge. It was the truth. It was what Mack D taught his men and his family. He was the Supreme Being. He was meant to rule. He was meant to have power and control.

He was always spewing today's mathematics or preaching to his young recruits. Mack D preached the Five Percent philosophy while simultaneously dealing drugs, murdering, and becoming one of New York's most dominant crime figures.

He took a timeout from his work and stared off into space. He thought about his son, and then Nichols flooded his mind. Two of his kids were dead—murdered! His little girl was beautiful, and so was Denise. He'd held Nichols a handful of times, but was far removed from her life. He was now sorry he couldn't be there for his daughter. He was also sorry to hear that Denise was dead too. But he didn't want to dwell on the past.

He focused back on his laptop, reading statements and numbers until there was a knock at the door.

"Come in," he said.

Richard walked inside.

Mack D closed his laptop and looked at him. "What's going on?"

"They're here."

"Okay, tell them I'll be up to see them in a few minutes."

Richard nodded. He turned to exit the office, but then turned back around. "Why play this cat-and-mouse game with these bitches and their niggas? I don't like it. It makes us look weak. We don't need any outside help. I can take care of every last one of them, Mack D. Just give me the word, and I'll paint the streets red with their blood—their children's blood too."

"Impatience can cause wise people to do foolish things."

Richard didn't respond. He always carried a stern face, never smiling. He was bred for war and handling the organization business. He was a cold person who had no problem doing what was necessary to get his point across. He had made his bones by becoming one of the deadliest men on the streets. He was Mack D's go-to guy whenever a problem surfaced. Richard was a cleaner—a cold-blooded killer in a suit and tie. He and Mack D had a long-term affiliation, having known each other since they were sixteen.

Mack D doused the cigar into the ashtray, then stood up from his chair, his long sleeves rolled up to his mid-forearms. He loosened the tie around his collared shirt and then moved from behind his desk. He stood in front of Richard and placed his hands on his shoulders, looking him in the eyes.

"My friend, trust me when I say this: I see the bigger picture in letting the sisters live for now, and the twin brothers," he said. "Remember this— revenge is a dish best served cold."

Richard started to speak, but Mack D continued with, "I loved my son, but he was hardheaded, especially for slacking out there in the streets when I told him about the danger. He took his life for granted; he always did. But, Richard, do not doubt that those responsible will hurt for this. The day will come when they think they're safe and suddenly their joy will turn to ashes in their mouths, and then you'll see that their debt has been paid."

Richard nodded.

"We should forgive our enemies, Richard, but not before they are hanged." Mack D laughed.

"Don't forget you have guests waiting upstairs." Richard pivoted and walked out the door.

Mack D lingered in the center of his office for a moment, staring at the closed door. He was left in silence to ponder the depths to which he would sink to get revenge. He went back to his desk and opened his drawer. He removed a new Cuban cigar, placed the cigar in his mouth, and exited his private office.

The provincial 1926 French castle where he resided had been brought into the twenty-first century with renovation and technology. The home boasted five bedrooms and four and a half bathrooms, plus a four-car garage.

The home was fit for a king. The minute anyone walked through the tall oak double doors with forged ironwork, they felt like they were inside a castle. The center hall opened off to the right into a huge living room accented by leaded glass windows, a beamed ceiling, and a raised stone fireplace adjoining a library, with wide-plank oak floors throughout. Then there was the sun-filled formal dining room with deep bay windows.

Mack D ascended the spiral staircase and stepped into the great room, where two men in dark suits and shades sat on his expensive VIG Chesterfield sofa. They had "NYPD detectives" written all over them. They both stood six-feet tall. One had short, black, cropped hair, and the other had a bald head and a salt and pepper goatee.

Detective Mogen was a fifteen-year veteran on the police force, while Detective Lowell was a ten-year veteran.

Mack D greeted them with a handshake. "Gentlemen, I'm sorry to have kept you waiting."

"Time is money and money is time," one of the detectives said.

"I agree wholeheartedly." He stood in front of the men and lit his cigar, taking a few deep pulls and enjoying the flavor of a good Cuban cigar, the smell lingering in the air. He exhaled. It was now time to talk business.

Richard stood off in the corner with his arms folded in front of him, his 9 mm holstered on his left side. He was against working with the NYPD, but like the twin situation, it was his boss's decision.

"Let's get down to business, shall we?" Mack D took a seat on the couch opposite of them. He nodded toward Richard, who approached with his signature scowl and handed Mack D a manila folder.

Mack D took the folder and passed it off to the detectives. The men opened it and looked at the glossy photos of three black men.

"I need them found immediately," Mack D said.

"For what reason?" Detective Mogen asked.

"I just need them found. That's all you need to know. Why and what I do with them is my business. I would hate to consider y'all accomplices."

Detective Lowell said, "You are a very funny man, Mack. But we'll find them, and our prices have just gone up. Twenty thousand."

"Twenty thousand." Mack D chuckled. "Inflation, huh?"

"Yes. You know our services don't come cheap."

"Yes, I see that. Twenty thousand it is."

Richard handed the men an envelope filled with cash, and Detective Lowell took the money.

"That's ten thousand there," Mack D said. "You'll get the rest when these men are found."

The detectives smiled.

"Consider them found," Detective Mogen replied.

"Also, I have more work for you two."

Detective Mogen nodded. "We're listening."

Mack D handed them two photos of Apple and Kola.

"Who are they?" Detective Mogen asked.

"I just need some information on them. I want to know everything about them, and I mean everything."

The cops stared at the photo.

Lowell commented, "Pretty girls."

"Who are they to you?" Mogen asked.

"Just two ladies that caught my interest."

Lowell smiled. "Your interest, huh?"

"I'll pay an extra ten thousand."

"That's fine by me," Mogen joked. "We love taking your money."

"Yeah, I bet y'all do."

Both cops had been on Mack D's payroll for two years. Whatever he needed, they got for him—information, people found, snitches he needed to know about. They would warn him of any investigations or potential indictments against him or his men. With moles inside the NYPD in his pocket, Mack D was always ahead of the curve.

The detectives stood up.

"Richard will escort you out," Mack D said, and the cops walked away.

Mack D took one more puff from his cigar as he stood in the great room. There was a lot to do and no time to waste.

EIGHT

Kola stood by the window and watched the children playing in the backyard. They were all smiles and laughter with no worries in their heart as they ran around in circles, tagging each other and falling to the grass. It was a delight to see them play. Children were so innocent.

Eduardo Jr.'s and Sophia's English had improved immensely. It felt great to communicate with them without Peaches being their translator.

Kola exhaled.

Kamel had taken them away from Brooklyn and moved them into a ranch-style home with a big yard on Staten Island. The house left a lot to be desired, but she'd lived in worse. It was dated yet cozy. The entry was protected with a recessed porch, and there was a large attached garage and large picture windows.

The suburban block was quiet. Across the street was a large, picturesque pond. The kids loved going there to feed the ducks and the swans some bread. It felt good to get away.

Kamel went to every length to protect his girlfriend and the children. He had procured an arsenal of guns, and he had his men watching the house and checking in on them frequently. Kola felt like she was in the witness protection program. But was all this necessary?

While gazing out the window at the children, she thought about Mack D. She knew if he wanted them dead, he could have killed them that day.

There had to be a reason why he didn't. She couldn't stop obsessing about it. Mack D was like a god in New York. He seemed to be everywhere and had resources far and wide. Were they really safe in some cozy home in Staten Island? If he had gotten to them once, wouldn't he be able to do it again?

All of a sudden, her cell phone rang out from across the room. She had no idea who it was. Not many people had her new number. She went to answer it.

"Hello."

"How's my family?" he spoke.

Hearing his voice sent chills throughout Kola's entire body. She stood frozen in the room, her breathing labored. It was Eduardo. *How did he get my new number?*

"Eduardo," Kola uttered, trying not to sound shocked to hear his voice. "I've been waiting for your phone call."

"You lying whore! I know what you've been up to. I know about your small-time hood boyfriend. Kamel, that's his name, right? You ready to die for him, or are you ready to watch him die?"

"Eduardo, what do you want from me?"

"You made a promise to me that you couldn't keep. I'm hurt, Kola. You lied to me. I hate that you lied to me."

"Eduardo, I didn't—"

"Shut up!" he screamed into the phone. "You think I wouldn't find you? You think you can run from me and be safe with your new boyfriend protecting you? Do you really think he can protect you from me, Kola? Do you think he can become me?"

Kola didn't know what to say.

"I sit here in this hellhole, and I still have power and wealth that Kamel can only dream of. It may feel like I'm across the world, but I can lay my hands on your shoulders at any given time, maybe move them up to your neck and snap it. Did you forget who I am? Did you forget what I'm capable of?"

"No, I didn't, Eduardo," Kola replied sheepishly.

"Your engagement, it's a slap in my face . . . after everything I did for you."

"I never planned on marrying him, Eduardo. It was only a ruse."

"I think you're a lying bitch. I know you're in love with him. I can hear it in your fuckin' voice. I can smell your deceit through this phone. I set you up, had you released from prison, and relocated you back to America. Nobody else is allowed to have you the way I had you. I miss you so much. I love you, Kola. I miss your touch, your smell, your sex."

"What do you want from me?" Kola cried out.

"I want him dead. I want you to suffer. I want you to feel pain, the same pain I feel not having you around. Since I can't have you physically, then I'll kill everything you love, starting with Kamel. You know with the snap of my fingers, I can have your precious little boyfriend lying face down in a pool of his own blood wherever he's standing."

Tears trickled down Kola's face. The thought of losing Kamel was devastating. She loved him in a different way than she did Eduardo. He was special; he treated her special.

Her heart felt faint. Eduardo's threats were real. She dropped into the armchair and took a deep breath. Her past was catching up to her. She couldn't panic, not now.

"I did everything for you, Eduardo. I did what you asked me to do, including keeping your kids safe. I gave them a good life here."

"You did. My gratitude is toward you. But you still betrayed me. You broke your promise when I kept mine. I gave you everything—money, shelter, jewelry, authority, and protection. When you came to me begging for my help, I gave you that help, and included your sister. I took you away to paradise. I gave you both new identities. I gave you a nice life."

"But I had to continue to share you with different bitches day after day. You had babies on me, Eduardo. You never gave me your fidelity."

He chuckled. "Oh, my infidelity, you cry about that, when any other woman would have loved to be in your position. They would understand the type of man that I am, and they certainly would look the other way and enjoy the life of a queen, everything at your beck and call."

Kola couldn't believe what she was hearing from him. Was he serious?

"But now you lose that life and you lose the man you love."

"I just wanted you to love me, and only me."

"And I will always love you. But you must pay for your betrayal."

How can he be such a demon?

"Now, let me speak to my children."

Kola took a deep breath. She went into the backyard, where the children were playing in the grass and dirt. She wished she could smile and laugh like them. To be a child again would be such a blessing.

"Eduardo Jr., Sophia, come talk to your father," she called out.

The siblings came running over happily. Kola handed Eduardo Jr. the cell phone. He couldn't wait to talk to his daddy. He was getting older and understanding a lot more. Eduardo Jr. spoke to his father in Spanish.

Kola stood to the side. After everything he'd said, she was still woman enough to allow the man to speak to his kids.

There was one thing for sure, though. She wasn't going to go out without a fight.

Kamel's black Denali pulled into the driveway and parked next to the silver Lexus. Kola stood by the window, watching Kamel climb out from the passenger seat. She was happy he was home. She felt alone without him, even though she had the kids around. There was nothing better than having the man she was in love with around.

Kamel's friend Maleek exited the driver side. Maleek was a bull of a man at six four, two hundred and eighty pounds with a beard. The man was a brick wall. He was security.

Kamel was on his cell phone while walking with confidence toward the front entrance, a shopping bag in his hand and a .45 tucked in his waistband. He looked handsome in his wool coat and fresh cut. He was always a trendy dresser.

The minute Kamel walked through the front door, Kola wrapped her arms around him and kissed him passionately. He kissed her back.

"I missed you," Kola said.

"I missed you too. Is everything okay?"

No, everything wasn't okay. Eduardo had called. He had threatened them. She was scared. But she didn't want to divulge that information to Kamel so soon. He needed to rest. He didn't need stress the minute he came home. Kamel was going through enough already.

"Yes, everything is okay," she replied softly.

"Where are the kids?"

"In the backyard playing," she said.

"I got them some gifts," he said, raising the shopping bag.

Maleek was standing in the doorway, his hulky figure like an eclipse blocking out the sun. He was there to protect the family, which was what Kola and Kamel called themselves—a family—no matter what was happening around them.

"Everything good here?" Maleek asked.

"Yeah, we good," Kamel replied.

Kamel walked deeper into the house with the gifts. He reappeared without them and went into the backyard, where the kids were playing.

Once the kids saw Kamel was home, all three quickly and excitedly ran his way with wide smiles. Peaches was the first to wrap her young arms around him, followed by Eduardo Jr. and Sophia. Kamel crouched low and hugged the children lovingly. Like Kola, he had fallen in love with them. He treated them like they were his own kids.

"Y'all been good today?" he asked.

"Yes," Peaches answered.

"That's my girl. You know, only good kids get a special treat from me."

"What you bring us?" Eduardo Jr. asked in his Colombian accent.

Kamel was impressed by Eduardo Jr.'s English. The siblings learned very fast. He smiled at them and said, "Y'all gifts. I hid them in the house."

"You did," Peaches said elatedly, clapping her hands together and jumping up and down.

The kids couldn't wait to see what Kamel had gotten them. In frightful times, it felt good to do something special for them. Kamel needed to take his mind away from the streets. The kids helped, and Kola helped a lot more with her late-night goodies.

"Go inside and find them," he said.

Peaches was the first to take off running past him. She rushed into the house like a gust of wind with the siblings right behind her.

Kamel stood to his full height. He was all smiles.

Kola was in the doorway, leaning against the frame, her arms folded across her chest. She was smiling. Seeing her man with the kids and his special way with them made her pussy wet.

"You know, you gonna spoil them," she told Kamel.

"I know, but you can't be the only one spoiled in this house."

"Oh, I can't, huh?"

"Nope, you can't," he said, his warm smile aimed her way.

Kamel pulled Kola into his arms and hugged her closely. He was always grabbing her into his strong hold, like a child clutching a teddy bear. He always made it known that she was precious to him. He couldn't get enough of her. He wanted to be close to her like he was her skin.

The two kissed again, this time more fervently and much longer. His hands roamed from the small of her back to the back of her ass. He squeezed.

She giggled. "You better stop."

"Why? You know what you do to me." He squeezed her ass tighter.

She could feel his erection growing against her. It was obvious he was in the mood.

In the neighbors' eyes, Kamel and Kola seemed like the perfect couple. He was affectionate and friendly, and she was doting and bright. Kamel looked like the hard-working father of three kids, and Kola looked like the loving housewife.

Kola had to pull herself from Kamel before things got too heated between them. She wanted him, but the kids were up and running around the house, and they had problems to discuss.

"Save some for tonight," she said.

"Damn, baby! I don't think I can wait until tonight. I want you now."

She giggled like a schoolgirl. "You got it that bad, huh?"

"I'm like a crack fiend," he joked.

Even in times of trouble, he found the time to inject humor into their lives. She laughed. She needed to laugh. She wanted to take her mind away from Eduardo calling earlier.

From inside the house, the two of them heard Peaches shout gleefully, "I found my gift. It's a Hello Kitty doll."

Peaches had become fascinated with Hello Kitty; they were her favorite toys. The siblings soon found their gifts hidden behind the couch—a teddy bear with giant bowtie around the neck for Sophia and Thomas the Tank train for Eduardo Jr. The children began playing with their toys all around the house.

"Where's my gift?" She hid her worries behind a wide smile.

"Your gift? You get that tonight."

"I bet I will."

The couple went into the house to be with the kids.

Maleek was close by; in fact, he was in the kitchen invading their fridge. He was always hungry.

While Kamel was engaged with playing with the children on the living room floor, Kola stood to the side and watched them. Increasingly, her smile morphed into a worried frown. It bothered her to see how great Kamel was with them. She didn't want this to end. She enjoyed the moment. She enjoyed the family living. But with Eduardo slinging deadly threats at her, it was hard to enjoy anything.

Kola disappeared from the living room. She needed a cigarette but didn't like smoking around the kids. She went into the kitchen, where Maleek was seated at the kitchen table chomping down on a ham, turkey, and cheese sandwich and throwing back a liter of Pepsi. His bottom swallowed up the entire kitchen chair.

She pulled out her full pack of Newports and lit one up. She took a needed drag, leaned against the sink, and asked Maleek, "Are you looking out for my man?"

With a mouth full of food, Maleek turned to Kola and replied, "I'm gonna always look out for Kamel. He's my boss."

She managed to smile. "You better, or you gonna have to deal with me."

"Don't worry. Where Kamel goes, I go, and with me, he's gonna always be safe," he said strongly.

She wanted to believe him, but she had seen what Eduardo's men and Mack D's thugs could do. Maleek had the size and the look, but did he truly have the skill and the heart? She wanted to protect her family. Kola wished that Superman was protecting her man, or she could become the man of steel herself and wipe out her foes with one death blow, take care of the problem, and get on with her life.

Kola prayed that one day she would have kids of her own with Kamel. She didn't want anyone else. This was it. He was the man she wanted to spend the rest of her life with. He was her soul mate, and he made her completely happy.

She took a few more pulls from her Newport as Maleek continued chomping down on his sandwich. She could still hear Kamel playing with the kids in the other room. His love was genuine. He would always spend time with the kids and her, no matter what was going on with his life. Somehow, he was able to put away the drama he was dealing with out in the streets. He was a man that didn't bring his work home with him.

Kola finished her cigarette and extinguished it with the tap water. She took a deep breath. Where do we go from here?

NINE

Kola stood by the bedroom window and gazed out at the night sky. The house was quiet. The kids were sleeping. From her open window, she could hear crickets chirping. The silence of the suburbs was soothing.

Maleek had left for home, and now it was just her and Kamel. It had been a good day so far. She was spending time with her man and the kids, and things seemed normal for now. But Kola knew all that could change in a heartbeat.

Her talk with Eduardo was still on her mind. She was frightened. If he had her new number, then there was a chance he knew her new location. How Eduardo was able to access information from a Colombian prison was a mystery to her. But he and his organization were always resourceful.

Kamel was in the shower. She wanted to join him, but she couldn't pull herself away from the window. She was smoking her umpteenth cigarette of the day. The bedroom was starting to smell like a chimney, but smoking calmed her nerves.

Another worry for Kola was not hearing from Apple. She'd called her sister's cell phone, but she wasn't answering.

Kamel walked into the bedroom with a white towel wrapped around his waist, and he was still wet. "You okay, beautiful?" he asked. He removed the towel and continued to towel off in front of her.

"Just standing here thinking about some things."

"What you thinking about?"

Kola turned and looked at her man glistening and looking too sexy. His manhood hung nicely, looking like a spectacle of art. He had a gift, in more places than one. It was distracting for a moment.

They'd promised to never hide anything from each other. So she had to tell him that Eduardo had called her.

"Eduardo called," she blurted out.

"What! When?"

"Today."

Kamel asked coolly, "What did he want?"

"He's not gonna go away." Kola looked frustrated.

Kamel sighed. He walked up to her. He looked into Kola's eyes with a straight-faced stare. He tried to keep cool. He wrapped his arms around her, trying to console her with his strength. He refused to show any weakness. "We just have to be extra careful with everything," he said.

"I know."

They stood by the window, looking outside into the backyard. Kamel was naked against her, her back pressed against his chest, his arms wrapped around her midsection, his towel on the floor.

"I'm here, baby. I got your back," he said with assurance. "They think we gonna keep running scared, but we ain't about that shit. I've been holding my own for a long time, never ran from anyone, and I'm not about to start now."

Kola managed to smile. It felt good to hear him say that, although she was still worried. Men like Mack D and Eduardo knew how to come at their enemies from different angles. You expect A, but you get C. They could get a man's best friend to turn on him. They had money to buy and influence people and had cemented themselves into position, building lasting connections in various places.

Kola understood that it just wasn't about holding their own out there. It was about being smart. Anyone could go out there and shoot guns. And then what? Niggas shot back too. When it came to the game, they had to move like a master chess player. One wrong move and they'd be dead.

"Ain't nobody gonna touch you or the kids," Kamel said. "I promise you that."

She heard him all the way. He said one thing, but Kola knew the truth.

She could see in Kamel's eyes that he was scared. She knew her man. Maybe he was more scared of Eduardo than Mack D. Eduardo was part of a ruthless cartel. He had made money that almost reached into the billions. He had people in every continent and was once on Interpol's list of one of the most dangerous men in the world.

"I love you," Kola said to him.

"I love you too," he replied happily. "I would die if anything would ever happen to you. You are my world."

She turned around in his arms to face him. His words were revitalizing. He looked at her with all the love and care in the world.

She smiled. "Let's forget about our troubles tonight and only focus on us."

He agreed.

She wanted to relax him. She could see the stress in his eyes—the grittiness of the streets almost swallowing him whole.

She took his hands and led him toward the bed. Gently, she pushed him down and removed her chemise before climbing on top of him. His manhood rose against her and came to attention as they touched.

She started from his neck with sweet, sensual kisses, went to his face, and then locked her lips with his. They kissed passionately. She started to stroke his shaft with one hand, while her other hand pushed against his chest. Kola's kisses traveled from his mouth to his chest, and she made her way down to his erect manhood.

Kamel waited patiently for the inevitable. She lowered her head, her lips parting. He watched as her tongue and mouth made his dick glisten. He groaned, "Mmmm! Shit!" He clenched his teeth.

She slid her lips up and down his big, hard dick. She worked faster with long, deep sucks, making him moan louder. She swirled her tongue around his tip and stroked him at the same time, and then she filled her mouth with it. She was trying to suck him dry.

Kamel squirmed. "You gonna make me cum," he announced.

That was the plan. Kola wanted her man to go somewhere special. She did her best with her hands and her lips, and she soon tasted his cum. She moaned onto his dick and welcomed the nectar spilling into her mouth.

Kamel moaned and quivered, tugging at her hair. He came hard, coating the back of her throat with his cum.

She crawled forward, smiling up at him, her breasts swaying.

He wrapped her into his arms and stared at her adoringly. "I love you so much," he proclaimed.

"I know you do. I love you too."

He held Kola against his naked frame. The room was quiet. He was still enjoying her nakedness and beauty.

They kissed, their tongues entwining, his hands cupping her butt. They accepted each other's hot kisses. Soon Kamel was rock-hard again. Kola wasn't done with him yet. Tonight, it was all about him.

"You ready for round two?" she asked with a teasing smile.

"I'm still recovering from round one," he joked, laughing, his dick throbbing under her touch.

She wanted to feel him inside of her. She straddled him, bringing his throbbing erection up to her wet pussy. She guided it into her.

Kamel thrust hard, sinking his dick deep into Kola, who clamped her eyes shut and whimpered in surrender as she rode his dick cowgirl-style—up and down, up and down. They both moaned agreeably.

Her hands gripped his shoulders tightly as they found their rhythm against each other and soon were kissing deeply as they fucked.

Her breathing became ragged. She was feeling the heat of an orgasm building inside of her belly. There was nothing better than pleasing yourself with your lover's body.

She gyrated on his fully erect penis as it stimulated her G-spot and clitoris to multiple orgasms. "Fuck me! Fuck me hard, baby! I want to feel you come!" Kola cried out as Kamel continued to plunge into her.

Moments later, her body became as hard as steel as Kamel thrust his dick deep as he exploded into her.

Kola collapsed on his chest and exhaled noisily. She snuggled against him and was able to laugh and smile. There was no way she was going to let this end.

Kola woke up with the morning sunlight percolating through the open blinds. She was naked under the white sheets. Kamel wasn't by her side. The bedroom was empty.

She propped herself upright against the headboard, her tits peeking from beneath the sheets. Last night was phenomenal. She'd wanted him to feel bliss—take her body completely. They'd made love for hours. Kamel had that young-man stamina. He kept going and going, and Kola loved it.

Kola wished that her family had a new life from every bit of danger that threatened to separate them. She blew air out of her mouth and removed herself from the bed. She donned a long robe and exited the bedroom.

The minute she stepped into the hallway, the smell of breakfast cooking wrapped around her nose like a lasso and pulled her in that direction. She walked toward the kitchen and heard the children.

Kamel was at the stove cooking breakfast for everyone. The kids were seated at the table, talking loudly in anticipation.

Kola stood at the kitchen's entrance. No one had noticed her yet. They were all too busy wrapped up in the aroma of breakfast cooking.

Kamel turned around with the spatula in his hands. He saw Kola and smiled widely. "Good morning beautiful," he greeted.

The kids removed themselves from the table and ran over to hug Kola. "Good morning!" they all greeted with smiles.

Kola hugged them back. "Good morning."

"You ready for breakfast?" Kamel asked.

"What you cooking?"

"Pancakes, eggs, and bacon."

"Sounds delicious."

"You gonna love it."

Kola gave him a morning kiss on his lips and then took a seat at the table. This was the life she wanted. But in the back of her mind, she couldn't stop thinking about Eduardo and Mack D. She knew these men could easily turn her dream into a nightmare. One day, Kamel could turn up missing, or he could be gunned down in the streets.

Kamel was cool and collected, for now. Kola felt responsible for that. Her sex last night could make any man forget about their troubles. Now how could she forget about her issues? That call from Eduardo really bothered her. Her threat alert was beeping on red, and her nerves were jumping like a firecracker.

Kamel finished making breakfast and made a huge plate for everyone. The pancakes were fluffy and tasty, and the bacon crisp and juicy. Everyone quickly devoured Kamel's cuisine. Kola had seconds.

After breakfast, the kids went outside to play, while Kola and Kamel remained in the kitchen to clean up.

While washing dishes together—He washed; she dried—Kamel smiled Kola's way and said, "This is nice. I like this."

"I do too."

"I'm glad we got out of the city and came here."

Distant for a moment, Kola's replies were short, but Kamel was talkative this morning.

"I had fun last night," he said.

"Me too."

"Maybe tonight, we can do it all over again. You know I'm lookin' forward to it."

She smiled.

Then he asked, "What's on your mind, baby? You've been looking kinda distant all morning."

"I was just thinking about a few things."

"Like what?"

Before she could get to answer, the doorbell rang.

"Hold that thought. Let me see who this is." Kamel walked out of the kitchen. Before he went to answer the door, he picked up his Glock 17, cocked it back, and moved cautiously to the door.

It was a wake-up call to the true life they were living.

With the gun in his hand, he glanced outside and looked relieved. "It's Maleek," he said to Kola.

Maleek was there to pick him up in the Denali so they could start their day. There was club business and drug business.

Kamel opened the door, and Maleek slid inside the house. He greeted Kamel with a fistful dap and a hood hug. "You ready?" he asked.

"Yeah, just give me a minute," Kamel replied.

Maleek hunched over and leaned closer to Kamel's ear and whispered, "We got an issue wit' ya twin."

"What kind of issue?"

"He ain't playing it safe. He's still on the streets, wilding the fuck out. Word got to me that he shot up some people's car after leaving the club the other night. No bodies, though."

Kamel let out a frustrated sigh. He was so sick and tired of his brother's wild antics. "Where is he now?"

"He at the old place, shacked up wit' the evil twin," Maleek said, referring to Apple.

"A'ight, I'm gonna go handle that."

Maleek nodded. He stood upright again.

Kola wasn't standing far from them. By their quiet discussion, she knew something was wrong.

"Good morning, Kola," Maleek said with a quick smile.

"Good morning, Maleek," she returned halfheartedly.

Kamel went toward his lady. He seemed unruffled about the news and about everything else happening. He stuffed the Glock into his waistband and snatched his jacket from the back of the chair.

"Everything okay?" Kola asked.

"Yeah, everything's cool."

"What did Maleek whisper into your ear? I'm no fool, Kamel. I come from the same streets as you. I know when something is wrong."

"Ain't nothing wrong, baby. It's my brother—he just an idiot."

"Is my sister with him?"

Kamel nodded.

"What's going on with them?"

"Just the same ol' stupid shit—not listening to advice, not tryin' to play it safe."

Kola could relate to how he felt. Apple was the same way. She didn't want to listen to any sound advice from anyone. Kola wanted her sister to come stay at the house, but Apple was on some reckless shit.

"Look, I'm gonna go and handle some business. You and the kids be safe. If you need anything, or if anything comes up, hit me on my cell phone." He gave Kola a quick kiss on her lips. "I love you." He walked out the front door with Maleek.

Kola went to the front entrance and stepped out onto the porch. She watched Kamel climb into the passenger seat of the truck. It looked like he was on his way to a nine-to-five, but it was after eleven a.m. She looked like an ordinary housewife saying goodbye to her husband who was off to his job while the kids were tumbling around in the playroom. It all seemed normal, but it wasn't.

The SUV backed out of the driveway and went left toward the freeway, which was miles away. Kola lingered on the porch and exhaled. She wondered if it would be the last time she saw him alive. It was a frightening thought. She shook the thought from her head and tried to remain positive.

It was a brisk morning. The neighbors surrounding her were either at work or running errands, and their kids were in school. Her neighbors didn't come around to be nosy. Kola liked that. The residents respected each other's privacy. There was no knocking on doors, greeting the new family on the block with warm hellos, or bringing cookies.

She looked around for a brief moment and went back inside. The children were still playfully rumbling and tumbling in the backyard, all buttoned up in their fall outerwear. Kola shook her head. She felt like a terrible parent. The kids should really be in school, but it was too risky with killers lurking around.

Kola went into her bedroom and opened her top dresser drawer. She retrieved a business card hidden underneath her clothing. She gazed at it and contemplated whether she should make the call or not.

No one but Kola knew Mack D had slipped his card into her pocket before they'd left the warehouse in the Bronx. He figured her to be the sensible one of the twins. She was tempted to call him to resolve their issues. She felt she needed to do something, especially with Eduardo being a threat. Maybe Mack D was the lesser evil. She was willing to risk her life if it meant keeping her family safe.

TEN

Jamel took a deep pull from the blunt between his lips as he exited the BQE, near the downtown Brooklyn area. Rick Ross was blaring in his smoke-filled Benz. He was living reckless, but he didn't care. His life was about having fun, getting money, fuckin' bitches, and doing him. He was doing that at full throttle. No one was promised tomorrow in life, so he was determined to make the most out of his todays.

He nodded his head to the fast and catchy track, "Hustlin'." Rick Ross wasn't one of his favorite rappers, but he loved the song. He loved hustling. Jamel had little respect for a correction officer rhyming about the street life. To him, the nigga was a fake—a studio rapper pretending that he lived that life of moving kilos and shooting guns. Jamel knew he was the real deal, and he would eat niggas like Ross alive.

But music was music, and if it was good, then he listened to it.

He didn't think about Apple at all. His mind was elsewhere. His pistol was near his reach, and with his tinted windows, he felt untouchable. Brooklyn was his home, and he drove around the area like he owned the streets.

Jamel cruised down Myrtle Avenue toward the Fort Greene section of Brooklyn. Soon, he came to a stop in front of the Walt Whitman housing projects on Myrtle and N. Portland Avenue. From the driver's seat he observed the block as he finished off the blunt. It was bustling on a sunny afternoon, with locals, drug fiends, and hustlers mixing about. There were a few cop cars patrolling the area and more cops on foot, walking through the projects, but Jamel wasn't concerned about the police.

The sprawling projects he sat parked in front of were once home to some notorious Brooklyn gangsters back in the days. Fort Greene was a section of Brooklyn you stayed away from if you had no reason to come around. Gunshots and violence were prevalent, and drug sales and users were an everyday thing. There was money to be made in Fort Greene.

Tito controlled the drugs and gangs there, and he'd run the area with violence and murder for years. He had been recently incarcerated with multiple indictments and was looking at a sentence of twenty-five to life. Now his underlings and a few young bucks were dying to fill his shoes and take over the area. Jamel wanted to take full advantage of the opportunity.

Jamel had befriended a hustler named Benny, a Blood member. Benny and Jamel were both money– and power-hungry and violent men. Benny was itching to become the next Escobar in the city, but he needed a connect. Jamel promised to hook him up with great quality dope and coke straight out of DC for the right price.

Jamel stepped out of his car with his pistols concealed on his person. Sometimes, he would carry two or three guns on him at a time. He wasn't about to get caught slipping on the streets. He wasn't worried about any stop-and-frisks by the police; he was so insane that if they threatened to search him, he would start popping off before they even came close.

He coolly marched toward the project building on N. Oxford Walk and entered the lobby. The elevator was taking too long, so he quickly ascended the concrete stairway toward the fifth floor and startled a crack whore giving a teen a blowjob for some drugs. It was nothing new to Jamel. He glanced at them and chuckled.

The young hustler looked no more than fifteen and had a horse-like penis. He looked warily at Jamel while he passed, and Jamel dared him with his eyes to say something disrespectful. He was ready to lay him down if the wrong words came out of his mouth. The teen said nothing, knowing real recognizes real, and Jamel's eyes spoke death.

Jamel went on his way, and the crack whore shoved the teen's big dick back down her throat. Nothing was going to get in the way of her high.

Jamel arrived on the fifth floor and walked toward Benny's apartment down the hallway. He knocked twice and waited. Jamel constantly checked his surroundings. His guns' safeties were off and they were cocked with rounds in the chamber. Every second mattered if something were to pop off.

"Yo, who that?" a voice from the other end asked.

"Jamel, lookin' for Benny."

The door opened, and a heavyset black male in a wife-beater with fuzzy facial hair faced Jamel. They looked at each other, sizing up each other's body language. Jamel wasn't intimidated by his size. He stood there looking poker-faced, waiting to be allowed inside the apartment. From where he stood, he could smell marijuana and hear the Xbox being played.

The man turned and shouted, "Yo, Benny, you got company."

"Who dat?" Benny shouted back.

"Some nigga named Jamel."

"Oh, let that nigga in, Tiny. He cool," Benny said.

Tiny nodded and stepped aside, allowing Jamel to enter before reclaiming his spot in the living room.

The place was a stash house and chill spot for Benny's crew. In the kitchen, two females were in their panties and bras cutting up and cooking a kilo of cocaine into street-ready vials of crack. There were guns on the coffee table, and Benny and another dude were in the living room playing Madden 14.

Benny was a short and stocky black male, late twenties and balding. His bare upper body was swathed with gang and prison tattoos. He rose from the couch with a blunt dangling from his lips and his jeans sagging and greeted Jamel with a dap.

"What's good, my nigga?" Benny said.

"Same ol', my nigga—'bout this money and business."

"I feel you, my nigga. I do. That's why we connect, yo," Benny responded in his hood tone.

Jamel nodded feebly. "I feel you."

Benny and Jamel locked eyes briefly. They shared a sub-zero coldness in their eyes. Benny was a predator in the streets of Brooklyn, and some considered him a violent bully. He grew up in Fort Greene and had a fierce reputation for preying on the weak and vulnerable. He took from everyone and shared nothing. He had a short temper and an itchy trigger finger. Now in his late twenties, either the streets or prison had been his home for most of his life.

Benny asked, "So, what's the word, my nigga? We good on business from DC?"

"Yeah. I hollered at my peoples, and they okay wit' it. Eighteen a key."

"Eighteen, huh? Yeah, that can work. I'm already paying twenty for some bullshit that I gotta cut like crazy just to make a profit. Ya feel me, my nigga? Fuckin' Dominicans in Washington Heights be tryin' to play a nigga. They lucky I don't run up in they spot and just take what I want. You feel me, my nigga? Right? Niggas gotta stick together and shit."

Jamel nodded again. He surveyed the apartment subtly. The wolves were mostly in the living room engaged in the video game and smoking weed. He noticed three 9 mm's on the table and two Glock 19s. He glanced into the kitchen and saw the two ladies seated at the table working. The apartment was sparsely furnished. It was two bedrooms, windows blacked out. It was perfect.

In Jamel's eyes, security was a little lax. Tiny had failed to search him at the door, and everyone inside was either working, getting high, or playing video games. Benny might have been a beast in this part of town, but Jamel felt he was the bigger and bolder wolf with sharper teeth.

Unbeknownst to Benny, there was no connect in DC. Jamel didn't have any peoples for dope or coke at the moment. Kamel was the brains and the king of networking. Jamel had gotten his product from Mack D, and since he and Mack D were at odds, Jamel's income was on pause until Kamel could find them another connect.

"You smoke, my nigga?" Benny asked him.

"Nah, I'm good," Jamel said.

Jamel was sick of him calling him "my nigga." He wasn't his nigga; they hardly knew each other. He was a wolf, and Benny was a wolf, and two vicious wolves trying to hang in the same pack never ended well. They both were hungry and ready to lead.

Benny lit the blunt that was dangling from his mouth. He took a deep pull and sat back on the couch. He was itching to do business with Jamel; it showed all in his face. Eighteen a kilo, he could definitely work with those prices.

Jamel took a seat nearby, and he and Benny started to discuss quality and quantity.

"I need the best, Jamel. I want that hundred percent pure quality coke. Ya feel me, my nigga? That's what ya peoples got in DC, right?"

Jamel laughed inside. Then he replied, "No one gets pure coke. Maybe if you go out and camp in Bogotá, Colombia and step on the coco leaves yourself, then maybe you get some pure coke. But what I got, it's eighty-five percent roughly. You cut it right, and you'll close the market in this bitch. But who knows? Maybe one day we'll get a few kilos of pure white straight from Pablo Escobar's grandkids and we'll look at each other and say, 'Let's go skiing!'"

Benny laughed. He didn't take any offense by it. He simply replied, "I like ya sense of humor, my nigga."

Jamel continued watching his surroundings. He put on a good act in front of everyone.

The two goons on the Xbox weren't paying him any close attention. They hollered at the video game, fingering the cordless game controllers rapidly.

Tiny shouted, "Yeah, nigga, fuck ya Cowboys! Fuck them niggas! They ain't fuckin' wit' my quarterback. Peyton Manning is gettin' in your asses, muthafucka! Touchdown, nigga!"

"Nigga, fuck you! Game ain't over yet!"

"Y'all niggas need to shut the fuck up!" Benny shouted, glaring at them. "Don't y'all hear me talkin' here?"

"Yo, I'm sorry, Benny. My bad," Tiny apologized.

"Yeah, we sorry, man," the other man followed.

"Yeah, y'all niggas is sorry, all loud over my business wit' Jamel. No fuckin' respect and shit—Matter of fact, get the fuck out the room! Bounce, niggas!"

The two quickly stood up and left the living room without any complaint. Benny eyed them heavily until they were gone.

The two girls in the kitchen heard the shouting and stopped working for a brief moment. Their pausing caught Benny's attention. He swiftly turned his wrath on them. "Yo, y'all bitches on a break?"

They looked at him dumbfounded.

Benny heatedly continued with, "Bitches, get back to fuckin' work bagging my shit! Fuck y'all sitting there lookin' at? Who told y'all to stop?"

They jumped back into bottling the crack cocaine.

Benny turned his attention back to Jamel and smiled. "Yo, sorry about that, my nigga. Just gotta keep shit straight up in here. You feel me, my nigga?"

"Yeah, I feel you, my nigga," Jamel replied matter-of-factly.

"So, let's finish talkin' about business."

"Let's talk about business," Jamel said, smiling.

Jamel spent no more than fifteen minutes inside the apartment but left with all the information he needed to stick up the place. It was going to be risky, but he loved the risks. Without risk, there weren't any rewards.

"Yo, y'all niggas pay close attention, a'ight?" Jamel hollered at his cronies inside the car. "We got one chance to pull this shit off, and I want it done right. We go in, we do our thing, and we out."

Everyone in the car nodded.

Jamel had plotted the whole robbery scheme. He had four men with him, each and every one of them ready to pull off the heist. They were a fearless group, not afraid to get in gun battles with other heavily armed drug dealers protecting their property. They needed the money, and they anticipated the thrill and the excitement.

Parked outside the Walt Whitman housing projects, the Lincoln Continental was roomy enough to host all five men. It was close to midnight, so there were few people outside. Jamel and his men were all dressed in black and sharing a cigarette while Jamel held court from the front passenger seat. He felt he had the perfect plan to infiltrate Benny's stash house.

"Mark-Mark, you take the lead into the apartment, and go about everything exactly as we planned. We gotta be quick and shit, and act like we're the real thing," Jamel said.

Mark-Mark nodded. "I'll be the real thing, all right."

Mark-Mark was a tall Caucasian male with a fit, muscular build. His body was fairly ripped. He exercised daily and was in top physical condition. He had a husky voice, wiseguy looks, and an authoritative aura.

"Mike, you right behind him, and you take control of the room," Jamel said.

Mike nodded. "I know what to do."

Mike was bald with a round face and small, sleepy eyes. Fresh home from a seven-year stint in Attica for assault and robbery, he was deadly.

The last two rounding out the group were Dennis and Bird, two young hoods from Brownsville who idolized Jamel and Kamel. Dennis and Bird looked up to Jamel like he was their big brother. Whatever he wanted or needed from them, they were quick to provide and implement.

"Yo, let's not fuck this up. That nigga got money up in that crib, and we want it, right?"

"Hell yeah, Jamel. I'm thirsty," Mike said. "My baby momma's already on my ass for fuckin' child support."

"Let's do this then," Jamel said.

The men climbed out of the dark blue Continental. Jamel popped the trunk, and Mike and Mark-Mark removed three large duffel bags.

They entered the building and took the stairway to the fifth floor. The elevator was too risky. Before they exited into the hallway, they all got ready for the assault. Each of them got dressed in what looked like DEA tactical uniforms—flight jackets and bullet-proof vests, along with fatigues, black ski masks, machine guns, and handguns equipped with silencers. Inside one of the duffel bags was an official police battering ram.

They positioned themselves in front of Benny's apartment door. Mark-Mark was the lead, gripping the battering ram and poised to strike the door. To anyone watching, it looked like Benny's place was about to be raided by the feds.

Mark-Mark glanced at Jamel, ready to receive the signal.

Jamel nodded. "Do it!"

Mark-Mark propelled the battering ram into the door, and it shook violently. The second strike sent the door flying off the hinges, crashing it open with a boom.

Everyone rushed inside.

"DEA! Don't move!"

"Don't fuckin' move! DEA!"

Two men were playing Xbox, Benny was on the couch, and Tiny was in the kitchen. Before Benny and his men could react, Jamel and his crew were all over the apartment with their guns pointed at everyone in the room. So far, Benny believed it was an official raid by the DEA.

"On the ground! Everyone, on the fuckin' ground now," Mark-Mark shouted.

Mike covered the living room and then stormed into the kitchen with his pistol directly in Tiny's face. He dared the man to move.

Benny and everyone complied with the orders given, so in seconds they had control over the apartment. Dennis and Bird made sure there wasn't a threat in the bedrooms, and Jamel had his Glock trained on Benny, who was face down on the floor, his arms spread out.

Benny shouted, "Yo, fuck y'all, man! Fuck the police!"

"What you say? Fuck the police?" Jamel approached Benny and kicked him in the face, drawing spewing blood and a cutting scream from him. Jamel felt good doing it.

Jamel and his men zip-tied everyone's arms behind their back and now had everyone in the room vulnerable.

"Where's the drugs and cash, my nigga?" Jamel asked, mocking Benny.

"Fuck you!" Benny shouted. He was able to glare up into his attacker's eyes. Then it suddenly dawned on him that it wasn't a real police raid and the men in the DEA outfits weren't real police.

"Yo, it's a setup!" Benny hollered. "They ain't fuckin' police!"

Jamel smirked and spat, "Stupid muthafucka! Yeah, we ain't police."

Jamel removed his black ski mask and revealed his identity. He gave the signal to Mark-Mark, and without hesitation, Mark-Mark put a bullet into the back of the head of one of Benny's goons.

The silencer muffled the shot.

Mark-Mark smiled.

The other captives squirmed.

"Drugs and money, nigga, where they at?" Jamel asked Benny again.

"Fuck you!"

Benny's defiance was becoming an annoyance to Jamel. He wasn't in the mood to play games. Jamel nodded, and quickly, another man in the room was executed.

"Two down, two to go," Jamel scoffed at Benny.

Bird and Dennis tore the apartment apart but didn't find anything. Time was critical. Jamel didn't want to spend too much time interrogating Benny. He wanted him to get the hint and break, but Benny was hardcore.

Benny continued glaring at Jamel and matched his scowl. "Fuck you!" he repeated.

Jamel's patience was wearing thin. His men continued searching desperately, rummaging through every room in the apartment. They were four minutes inside.

Jamel continued to hold Benny at gunpoint.

Tiny was executed. The bullet tore through his skull, and his body fell limp on the floor with his arms tied behind him and his crimson blood pooling around him.

Mike frantically looked through the kitchen. Suddenly he shouted out, "Bingo!"

Everyone's attention turned toward the kitchen. Mike pulled out three kilos of cocaine and close to one hundred thousand dollars in cash concealed inside a secret compartment in the stove.

Jamel smiled. It was gold. They hurriedly bagged what they came for. Subsequently, they murdered Benny, leaving behind no witnesses.

ELEVEN

The Denali pulled into the driveway of the Staten Island home and came to a stop. Kola was already staring out the doorway, knowing it was Kamel arriving. As a precaution she kept her pistol close. It was hard to see through the tinted windows, but she was sure everything was copasetic.

The kids were in their bedroom, the family movie *Rio 2* occupying their attention. They were fed, bathed, in their pajamas, and ready to go to bed soon. Kola had had a long and eventful day with them. When Kamel wasn't around, they kept her sane. They kept her company and gave her a purpose. Now, she wanted to spend some more quality time with her man.

It was a calm and quiet night on the block, just the way she liked it. The moon was full and bright. The night dropped over the suburbs like a heavy curtain freckled only by the fewest of stars.

The passenger and driver's door opened up to the Denali, and Kamel and Maleek stepped out of the truck. Then the back door opened. Kola was shocked to see they had company. She wasn't expecting to see Apple, but there she was, walking behind Kamel and his personal bodyguard.

Kola smiled, happy to see her sister. Finally, they were together again. She'd been worried about Apple. She wondered how Kamel convinced her to come to Staten Island.

Kola was grateful. Apple and Peaches were the only biological family she had left.

The second Apple walked into the house, Kola wrapped her arms around her sister and embraced her lovingly. "I'm glad you came, Apple."

"So this is home now," Apple said, looking around.

"It is. It's safe for now, until we find something more permanent and secure," Kamel chimed.

"Where's my daughter?" she asked.

"She's in the bedroom with Sophia and Eduardo Jr. watching cartoons."

"I need to see her. I miss my baby. Peaches!" Apple called out. "Peaches!"

Peaches came out the bedroom and saw her mommy. She ran her way with open arms and gave her mother a loving hug that felt like it would last forever.

The siblings were happy to see Apple too. She'd never treated them unfairly. Apple was fun and fond of them. The life she lived on the streets didn't surface around them. She hugged the siblings too, and it felt good to be around the children.

"I missed you, baby girl," Apple said to her daughter.

"I missed you too," Peaches said, sweetly. "I love you momma."

"I love you more," Apple replied.

Kola stood close by, watching the reunion with a slight smile. It was good to see her sister developing into a mother to her child.

It was a beautiful fall day with the sun bright and high in the sky. The weather was picture-perfect. The sky was blue and limitless.

Apple sat in the lawn chair with a blanket on the back porch sipping on hot tea and talking to her sister. The kids were running around in the backyard, playing with the fallen leaves and having fun like always. Kamel wasn't home, so Kola and Apple had some quality time to spend with each other.

Apple fixed her eyes on her daughter momentarily; her daughter was the apple of her eye. Peaches was so playful and energetic. Apple wanted her to stay like that forever. She didn't want her to go through any of the hardship and poverty that she, Nichols, and Kola went through. Growing up, they were poor and abused and had to do whatever necessary to survive living in the ghetto. Denise was never a doting mother to any of her kids and was never there for them.

Apple sighed and took a sip of tea. The sisters were enjoying a moment of tranquility, the afternoon sun in their faces coupled with a mild breeze from the east.

Then an upsetting thought crept into Apple's mind. Peaches was a beautiful little girl. She didn't look like Apple, though. Apple wondered if she was starting to look like her father, whoever he was.

Taking her eyes off Peaches and looking at Kola, Apple said, "When she starts asking about her father, what am I supposed to tell her?"

"The truth," Kola replied.

"Sceriously, Kola, you know how much my truth hurts. I have no idea who he is. I was turned into a fuckin' whore in Mexico, and her father is some damn trick that slipped a nut inside of me while I was drugged and vulnerable."

"It wasn't your fault, Apple. Everyone that was responsible for that is now dead."

The nightmare would forever be burned into her mind and soul. Apple hated to think about that time. Peaches was the only good thing that came out of that tragic season of her complicated life.

"We all been through hell and back, Apple. Look around you and just enjoy a slice of heaven for once. We're still here, and everyone that came against us is not."

Apple didn't respond.

Kola added, "Peaches is a blessing, no matter how you look at it, sis. She's your future; she's our future. And when she asks about her father, you tell her the truth. We are a family that doesn't sugarcoat our history. We came a long way, and nothing is going to beat us. You hear me, sis? Together, we're stronger than ever."

Apple sighed again. To her, it was easier said than done. Apple felt she went through more pain and more tribulations than her sister. Kola never had her face scarred. She wasn't forced to become a prostitute in Mexico, raped, drugged, and beaten. She didn't have the guilt of Nichols' death on her soul. Apple had been through so much shit, she could write a best seller, and her book would probably make The New York Times' list.

The only thing the sisters hadn't dealt with was doing serious prison time. Fortunately, they had escaped lengthy incarceration. They had to stay low-key and remain smart. They were still wanted by the FBI. One mistake could cost them their freedom.

Apple knew she and Kola couldn't afford to be locked up. It would put Peaches in foster care, and Apple would rather die than have that happen.

"We just have to stay focused on us and the kids. This is nice right now, but you know we still have threats out there," Kola said.

"I know."

Kola always kept it real, and she was forgiving about all that had happened between her and Apple. The past was their past. She was mainly focused on their future together.

"Thank you for finding her," Apple said.

"You don't need to thank me again, Apple. She's my niece, and I love her too. We was going to find her, even if we had to turn this world upside down and create chaos."

Apple smiled. She raised the cup to her lips and took another sip of tea. The past couple of days were different for her. She had time to relax and think. She was itching to roll up and light up somewhere private. Kola smoked too, but nowhere near as much Apple's new habit, and Apple didn't want her sister judging her.

Apple suddenly said, "I went to the grave the other day and saw Nichols."

Kola sat quietly. Nichols' death was a painful memory for them both.

"I had to go and see her. I know it's been a while, but I said my piece and I apologized to her, Kola. It was hurtful, but I knew it needed to be done."

Kola nodded. "I guess it did." Kola had been to the grave a few times and spoken to her sister. She felt her humbling presence whenever she stood over her grave. Nichols' memory made her forgive Apple.

The subject soon went from Nichols to their awkward situation with Mack D.

Kola handed Apple his business card.

Apple quickly saw the name and wanted to tear it up. "What is this? Why do you have his card, Kola?"

"He slipped it into my pocket that night in the warehouse. I just held on to it, just in case."

"Just in case what? You thinking about calling him? Are you out of your fuckin' mind?"

"Maybe we can talk to him, see if what he has to offer us is for real, a truce with him. I mean, he was once our stepfather, and he was Nichols' biological father."

"And you think that shit means something to me? It don't, Kola. I don't trust him at all. I don't care what he says to us. He's trifling, and he is not to be trusted. Think, Kola, Jamel murdered his son. Don't be naïve. That nigga is up to something."

Kola still thought there was hope with Mack D, and that maybe he was willing to allow the twins back into his life without any repercussions.

"You always been smart, Kola. Don't start thinking idiotic now."

"I plan to be careful around him."

"So you've already made up your mind? You can't be fuckin' serious, Kola! No! Stay away from that fuckin' man!" Apple screamed out, causing the children to stop playing and look over in the direction of the sisters.

"I'm sorry for cursing, y'all," Apple said to the children. "Me and auntie are just having a little disagreement. Y'all keep on playing."

Apple looked at Kola and felt disappointment. Why was she even entertaining the idea of reaching out to a monster like Mack D?

"Do you remember him, Kola, who he was back then and how he treated our mother? He was a piece of shit back then, and he still is now. He wasn't even in Nichols' life; he was just a sperm donor."

Kola had actually already talked to Mack D. The two had had a decent conversation via phone. He seemed believable, like he had some regret about the past and wanted to make up for it somehow. Kola wanted to believe he was legit with his truce and was willing to take a chance. In some warped way, she was somewhat delighted to have a parent back in her life. Mack D was hood-rich with the right influences. It was a stretch to connect with him, but maybe it was a risk that could save their lives.

The sisters sat outside talking all afternoon. Conversation became intense when they talked about their past and Mack D, but it didn't boil over. Apple and Kola wanted to do things differently and be different. Fighting and arguing with each other was stupid, so they knew how to talk out their issues and become better women.

Later that evening, Kamel showed up and walked into the backyard to join the sisters and the kids. The minute he set eyes on Kola, his whole face lit up with love. They never got tired of each other. The first thing he did was kiss his woman on the lips.

He said to her, "I missed you, baby. How was your day?"

"Better, now that you're here," Kola replied.

Apple sat and watched their love shine bright like the North Star in the sky. What they had together was priceless. She wanted the same thing with Jamel, but he was a lost and chaotic cause. Why couldn't her man be like his twin brother? Though identical in appearance, they were two completely different men on the inside. She felt a little jealous. Kola always had the good ones—Cross, Eduardo, and now Kamel.

"I'm gonna let y'all two lovebirds be," Apple said, standing up all of a sudden.

"You leaving us?" Kamel asked.

"I'll be inside."

Apple needed to get lifted. She excused herself from the backyard and went into the bathroom, where she rolled and lit up some Kush.

TWELVE

Kola woke up early and got dressed in a pair of tight jeans that accentuated her hips and ass, a long-sleeve designer top under a belted fall jacket, and designer heels that made her four inches taller. Her sensuous hair reached down to her shoulders, and she applied just the right makeup to emphasize her beautiful features even more. The kids and Apple were still sleeping, and Kamel was in New Jersey taking care of some business, so she had some time to move around. She had already called a cab and placed her .380 in her purse. She was ready to go.

Before she walked out the front door and headed toward the idling cab, she left Apple a note.

I'll be gone for a moment. Please watch the kids. I left to handle some business. Love y'all, Kola.

She pinned the note onto the fridge, where Apple would eventually see it.

With the sun brand new and fresh in the sky, she walked outside and climbed into the cab.

"Where to, ma'am?" the driver asked.

"I'm going into the city, downtown."

The driver nodded. It was going to be a costly trip. He put the cab in gear and slowly drove away from the curb.

Kola stared out the window from the backseat, hoping she was making the right choice. Mack D had invited her and Apple to have dinner with him in his mansion. Kola was reluctant to go at first, but she had a plan.

The cab crossed over the Verrazano Bridge into Brooklyn, taking I-278 through Brooklyn and then crossing the Brooklyn Bridge into Lower Manhattan.

The traffic was thick during morning rush-hour, but Kola wasn't in a hurry. She had plenty of time before her dinner with Mack D. Mack D was sending a car to drive her to Long Island from her place in Lower Manhattan.

She sat coolly in the backseat and enjoyed a cigarette while the driver navigated his black cab through the downtown city streets. There was a lot to think about and more to worry about, but Kola refused to dwell on the negative. She'd taken chances before, and they had paid off. But was she pushing her luck?

The cab came to stop at the building. The fare was sixty-five dollars.

She handed the man a hundred dollar bill. "Keep the change."

"Thank you. Thank you so much."

Kola climbed out of the cab and walked toward the lobby entrance. The sidewalk was swamped with people on their way to work. She strutted inside and took the elevator to her apartment. Before she entered, she pulled out her pistol and made her way into the apartment. It had been two weeks since they'd been there. Nothing looked unusual.

She checked every room, and everything appeared to be the way they'd left it. She set the gun on the kitchen table and looked inside the fridge. She was famished, but almost everything in the fridge was either spoiled or needed cooking. She made a turkey sandwich and watched television for hours in the spacious living room.

Kola lingered inside the apartment, smoking a cigarette while waiting for the phone call from Mack D. She sat near the large living room window gazing down at the city street.

It was turning out to be another beautiful fall day. Life below was flowing freely, and the sidewalk was bustling with foot traffic. It looked like everybody had somewhere important to be—maybe work, maybe school, or maybe to meet a friend in a café or a park. They damn sure weren't waiting for a private car to pick them up to meet with a drug kingpin.

"I wish things could be simple," she said out loud to herself.

She took a drag from the Newport and blew out a cloud of smoke. She was anxious. She tried to clear her mind from any worries and think about her family. The .380 she carried was minor protection, but what good was it going to do against machine gun-carrying henchmen that would kill for Mack D with the snap of his fingers? *I might as well be carrying a slingshot,* she thought, feeling like David going up against Goliath.

She took another pull from the cigarette as she sat alone in the empty apartment. She thought about Eduardo. She hadn't heard from him since he'd called and threatened her.

Her cell phone rang. It was Apple calling.

Kola answered, "Hello?"

"Kola, where are you?"

"I'm in the city, taking care of something important. I won't be long, sis. I just need to do this."

"Do what, Kola? What made you get up so early in the morning and leave me here with the kids?"

Kola was silent. She didn't want to tell her sister why she'd left.

Apple was no fool. She quickly deduced why her sister left in the morning without telling anyone. "You stupid bitch! You gonna meet with him, aren't you?"

A deep breath spilled from Kola. "I need to do this, Apple, for many reasons you wouldn't understand."

"Explain it to me then. Make me understand."

"If I can get Mack D to trust me, I can take him out if push comes to shove."

"How? You got an army behind you?"

"Not at all. Heart and opportunity is all I need. You know this."

"Yeah, but he's a sneaky muthafucka, Kola. I know the type. You can't get up close in an intimate setting because he'll see the hit coming from a mile away. Mack D has to get snuffed out in an ambush."

"And risk him escaping the hit?" Kola didn't allow Apple to answer. She continued, "When I go after him, I need to know he's dead. Then, and only then, do we ambush all his goons because they will definitely retaliate."

Apple exhaled. "You're sounding like the old Kola."

"Don't get too excited. There's a flipside to the game. Murdering Mack D is the last resort."

"I can't believe I'm hearing this!" Apple was heated. "That nigga had us both beat the fuck up. And don't forget he had a gun on my daughter!"

"Look, we both got into this game knowing all the risks. We learn from our mistakes and move forward. We're no longer teenagers, living reckless. We both got shit to live for, so if Mack D can't play nice then he dies. But if I could get him on my side, on our side, then so be it. No war."

"You think Mack D is gonna put together one big happy family and play nice suddenly?"

"Look, Apple, we talked, and he invited us to dinner at his place. I knew you wouldn't come, but I accepted. It's my choice, so stop worrying. Remember, we don't run from anyone, and we hold our own wherever."

"Did you tell Kamel about this?"

"You know I didn't." Kola knew Kamel would have agreed with Apple.

"He would have gone upside your head, like I should have done. I knew you was going to do something crazy like this."

"Remember, he could have killed us when he had the chance."

"I don't understand this, Kola. It's a stupid risk you are taking. And for what?"

"For us."

"We could have handled this in a different way."

"I feel this is the only way, Apple. I trust my decision."

"Kola, just be safe and keep your cell phone on. And do you know where this dinner is happening?"

"I don't. Just that it's on Long Island."

Apple sighed.

Just then, there was another call beeping in on Kola's phone. The caller ID said unknown. She said to Apple, "I need to take this. It might be him."

Before Kola clicked over to answer the call, she heard Apple blurt out, "I love you, sis. Be careful."

"I will."

Kola answered the second call coming in. "Hello."

"The car will be there in ten minutes," Mack D said. "Be ready and don't keep them waiting." He hung up.

Them? Kola wondered who "them" was.

Could she change her mind and turn back and go home? She didn't want to. In her mind, there was too much at stake, and she wasn't the type to back out of anything. When her mind was made up, she hardly changed it. She collected herself and exited the apartment.

Outside the building a black Mercedes-Maybach S600 pulled up to the front entrance. The driver stepped out, quietly walked around the car, and opened the back passenger door for Kola. She scanned the inside of the car, and he was alone. There was no Mack D or armed thug to escort her inside the vehicle. So why had Mack D said "them?"

She slid inside the backseat, and the door was shut.

It wasn't her first time inside a Maybach. She was accustomed to the finer things in life because of Eduardo. The sleek chariot was loaded with over-the-top features like massage chairs, interactive technology via touchpads and a glovebox for perfume. The real party was in the backseat, where there was enough space to fully recline, two champagne glasses ready to go, and a refrigerator in the back centerpiece. Not to mention TVs and adjustable footrests.

The Maybach moved away from the curb and merged into city traffic. The driver remained quiet. It was going to be a long ride from Manhattan to Long Island. She lit a cigarette and kept her cool.

Sixty-five minutes later, the Maybach came rolling to a stop in front of a lavish castle-like mansion in a ritzy neighborhood in Old Westbury, Long Island. The place kind of reminded her of one of Eduardo's compounds in Colombia. Two armed suit-and-tie men in black were standing at the front entrance, their weapons holstered underneath their jackets.

The driver stepped out of the Maybach and hurried around to open Kola's door. She stepped out and looked around. The place was sprawling and gated. Her heart started to beat faster. She clutched her purse close to her. The men standing by the front door looked her way with a blank stare.

"Follow me, ma'am," the driver said to her.

He walked ahead. She followed. They climbed the short stairs, and one of the henchmen opened the front door.

Before she could step inside, he said, "Spread your arms and hand over your purse. It's procedure."

She didn't have a choice. She handed him her purse. "I'm carrying, a .380."

While one carefully frisked her, not shying away from her ass and tits, the other went through her purse and removed the pistol. So much for her protection.

"I had to try, right?" She'd figured they were going to search her anyway.

He plainly looked at her. His reaction was stoic. "She's cool."

She walked through the iron high-brow doors and into the home. The driver stood nearby.

Kola felt some trepidation. She kept her guard up, but understood she was vulnerable with no gun, deep in Long Island with no transportation or help.

"Where is he?" she asked the driver.

"He'll be around shortly," the driver responded.

He was detached and not saying too much. Kola looked at him, clean-shaven and dressed in his suit and bowtie. He looked like a Muslim. He stood behind her like a statue in the room.

I don't have all day, Kola said to herself. Whatever Mack D was up to, she didn't want to wait around for it.

Just then, Richard walked into the room where she was standing and trying to look calm. He looked her way with a dark frown. His presence made her uneasy inside. She remembered him from the warehouse. He was the driver, and he'd kept the kids away. She remembered him saying something to Mack D concerning their fate, and it was obvious he was his right-hand man. His menacing eyes were fixed on Kola, and she couldn't read him.

They locked eyes. Kola wasn't about to give him the satisfaction of looking intimidated by him.

"I didn't come here to wait all day," she said to Richard. "I came a long way to talk to Mack D, not stand around like I'm some piece of furniture."

He didn't respond. He just stood there like a soldier on guard, with his arms folded in front of him. He was built like a Rottweiler—Mack D's guard dog standing at attention. She knew he was armed.

"What's your body count, huh? Ten, twenty, fifty maybe? How many men did you kill for your boss?" she asked boldly.

He didn't respond.

"I was just trying to make conversation," she said with quick sigh. "I guess the only talking you do is with your pistol, huh?"

Still no response from him.

Muthafuckas were getting on her nerves. Her patience was wearing thin, and she wasn't in the mood to be toyed with. She might have been unarmed, but her tongue was still sharp and her mind cunning. If push came to shove, she knew she could rely on her gift of gab, or maybe her sexuality to get a nigga open.

The place was huge and nicely decorated with antique furnishings and fine artwork. She decided to walk around the living room and scope it out. Before she could take three steps, Richard suddenly said something to her.

"You need to remain in this room only, until Mack D tells you otherwise," he said.

"Oh, now you fuckin' talk. For a minute I thought you was a mute."

She didn't get a reaction from him still. He remained expressionless and unmoving, and he kept his distance from her.

She shook her head from side to side and laughed to herself. "I hope your boss is more fun to talk to." She had to lighten her mood and think positive.

Kola took a seat on the couch and continued staring at Richard. He was a handsome man, but his demeanor was chilling like an Antarctic ice lake. The thought she had that maybe one day he would kill her, or she would have to kill him, wasn't comforting at all.

"Excuse the prolonged wait," she suddenly heard Mack D say. "I had some business to take care of inside my office. Money never sleeps."

Kola stood up and looked his way. He walked into the room dressed sharply in a three-piece suit and a fedora with the feather on the side. He looked a blend of a Wall Street broker and a pimp.

He smiled and extended his hand to hers. They shook hands, with him saying, "It's nice of you to come. I'm glad you accepted my invitation."

Kola's heart couldn't stop beating rapidly. She was nervous, but it didn't show. On the outside, she could hold out her hand and it wouldn't shake.

"I had the impression that your sister would come too. What happened?"

"She couldn't make it. She had a prior engagement."

Mack D looked disappointed. "How sad. I wanted her to be here too. I wanted to talk to both of y'all. I'm upset and I feel disrespected that she couldn't cancel her prior engagement to have dinner with her father."

"Stepfather, or once was," Kola quickly corrected him.

He smiled. "Yeah, it's been a long time. But must I remind your sister that not too long ago, her life was in my hands, and now she spits in my face by declining my invitation for dinner."

"I'm here," Kola said.

"Yes, you're here. One out of two, huh? So shall we go elsewhere and talk, catch up on long lost time?" Mack D said, stretching his hand toward another connecting area the dining room.

Kola walked into the dining room, and Mack D was behind her. She was still edgy. She still had no idea why he asked to see her. Why was he being so different? So strange?

Inside the dining room, Mack D lit a cigar and said, "Have a seat. You don't need to worry, Kola. You're in good hands. If I wanted you dead, then I wouldn't have chauffeured you to my home. Besides, you're family."

He did make a point. But they weren't really family. Far from it!

The room she was in was ritzy with a crystal chandelier above and stationary drapery panels with fringe hanging from decorative knobs. The walls were ocher, and the cedar bookcases provided a pop of color in the form of art and picture frames and housed the sound system. There was a wood slab dining room table in the center that featured a natural uncut bark edge. Long taper candles illuminated the table, and Mack D's staff was standing by, waiting to serve dinner.

"Have a seat and enjoy my hospitality," he said.

Kola took a seat at the table, and Mack D sat opposite of her.

Richard walked into the room and whispered something into Mack D's ear. He made Kola uncomfortable. Mack D nodded, and Richard stepped out of the dining room, leaving the two alone with the staff to serve them.

Mack D looked at Kola and said, "As you can see, I give nothing but the best."

Then he went on to give her a little information about the area his home was in.

"Did you know that Old Westbury is the richest town in the United States? The Hamptons is the ghetto, compared to this place. I picked this area to live because of its history. This place is famous for being the home of many of New York's and America's wealthiest families, including the Vanderbilts and Du Ponts."

"I didn't know that," she replied.

This wasn't the same man she remembered when she was a small child. He had changed a lot. Kola remembered him as a simple-minded thug that would come and dick down her moms. Domencio hardly had two nickels to rub together and was one of the dumbest criminals Denise had ever fucked. Kola was baffled he could turn out to have all of this.

She wished Nichols were alive to benefit from her father's come up. Domencio got Denise pregnant and was seldom around to co-parent. He never bought diapers, baby formula, or took his daughter school shopping. Now he wanted to brag about fine wines and Du Ponts.

"You see, during my time in prison, I did a lot of reading, and I bettered myself. I became part of something powerful, and I educated myself to Allah. I'm embarrassed to remember who I was back then. But my past doesn't define me now."

Kola had a hard time accepting that a man like him could become a Five Percenter. It seemed dated.

"I hear you're a Five Percenter now."

"I am."

"I guess Buddhist or Christian was all taken." Kola chuckled.

Mack D was not as amused. "Perhaps so."

Kola was tiring of the small talk, nor did she care to hear about how he'd changed. "Why am I here, Mack D? Let's be frank—your son is dead because of Jamel, and now you want to accept us into your home? What kind of game are you playing?"

"No game, Kola. My son wasn't like me. He was careless. His death was inevitable."

"So you expect me to believe that you forgive Jamel for what he's done? Really?"

"Listen, I didn't come here to talk about my son's death. I put that behind me. I invited you and Apple here to talk about us."

"And what is us? Where do we go from here?"

He smiled. "You are the precocious sister—I admire that."

"I grew up learning not to trust people and to always watch my back."

She didn't believe he put his son's death behind him. There had to be a motive, but she couldn't read him. He was a nut that wouldn't be easy to crack, but she had her own motives. It was going to take skills to pull it off, if it was feasible.

"You're a survivor, Kola, like me. You were able to adapt to any environment."

Mack D placed the cigar into his mouth and took a few pulls. The cigar smoke lingered around him like a thick fog. "You mind if I smoke?"

"It's your place."

"Do you drink?"

"Occasionally," she replied.

He nodded to one of his servants, and she approached the table. Mack D said to her, "I want you to get a bottle of red wine, the vintage stuff. The Domaine Leflaive Montrachet Grand Cru."

She nodded and then hurried toward wine cellar.

"You're going to love this stuff. It's expensive, but it's worth every penny."

Dinner was soon served. The table was decorated with an appetizing steak, potatoes, cabbage, and fried okra.

Kola sipped on red wine and enjoyed the food.

A discussion started to brew between them.

"Tell me how she died, your mother?"

It was a painful reminder for Kola. "It's a long story."

"I have time."

"She was murdered by one of our enemies, but they're all dead now," she said, almost making a statement. She vaguely went on to explain the events that led to her mother's demise.

Mack D listened, sitting there deadpan. He then said, "I remember when I first met your mother. She was something else. She had my heart, I admit. Y'all were babies then."

Kola took a sip of the wine. It helped her to relax. She started to talk more. She went on to tell Mack D a little about her and Apple's life.

"We went through a lot," she said to Mack D, hoping to gain empathy.

"I can believe it."

She started to talk about her sister. She told him about Apple's hard life, mentioning Chico, and then briefly bringing up Supreme and Guy Tony. She told him how bitches had always been envious of them. And then she mentioned the acid incident with Apple.

Mack D listened intently. The twins' lives were better than a daytime soap opera.

But Kola wasn't about to tell him the full story. She figured if she started talking, opening up to him to some extent, then he would trust her and she could get closer to him. She was telling him just enough to neutralize the bad blood between them. It was a sob story.

She didn't tell Mack D that Denise had paid someone to toss acid in her own child's face. Nor that Apple had Chico murder her best friends. She also didn't tell him that subsequently, the brother of the slain girl had gotten his revenge by selling Apple to a whorehouse in Mexico. No, all of that was left out of the conversation. She wanted Mack D to feel some type of sympathy for her sister.

Then she told him her own sob story. She talked about Cross, his baby momma, her conflict with Apple, and finally Eduardo. She talked about her battles with men. The wine kept flowing, and Kola continued talking.

"You are a survivor. How did you escape prosecution in the States?" he asked.

"Eduardo. He took me and my sister in. He changed our identities and made us disappear. Do you know him?"

"I don't know him personally, but he's well known."

"Well, anyway, I fear for my life now and Kamel's too."

"Why?"

She told him the story about her sudden escape from Colombia.

He then said, "I told you, you are now protected by me. No one will bring any harm to you or your family. No one is going to fuck with you or your kids."

Kola was skeptical. It sounded good, but was it true?

Mack D felt the timing was right. "Let's lighten the mood, shall we?" He called for Richard, who brought in two huge boxes. "For you and Apple."

Kola was taken aback. "Wait. What?"

"Gifts for my daughters," Mack D announced, proudly. "These are custom made."

She stumbled. "I can't—we can't."

"Kola, don't be rude. I went through a lot of trouble finding the perfect gifts for my twin girls. Please, open them, as a peace treaty."

It was more of a demand than a statement.

Kola opened the first box while Mack D gleamed with pride. It was a purple mink coat. The second box held a red one. She was speechless.

"You're welcome," said Mack D, sarcastically.

"Oh, my bad. Thanks. It's more than we deserve so early on."

"But not more than you're used to?"

"Exactly."

For some reason Mack D was irritated that Kola wasn't more impressed with his gift. Since he'd come up in the drug game, his money had bought loyalty, dick-riders, hoes, respect, goons, thugs—the whole nine. Yet Kola's mouth said, "thank you" and her eyes said, "big deal."

"Which one do you like best?"

She looked from purple to red. "I'll give the red to Apple. It's more her personality."

"Good. It's settled then. Have more wine."

It was late evening when Kola left, the two mink coats in tow, knowing that everything came with a price.

With all the drama in her life, was she for sale?

THIRTEEN

J amel's latest caper was all over the news, making the front pages of newspapers. Fox 5, NY1, and UPN all covered his handiwork.

Breaking news: *"Four men were found dead in an apartment at the Walt Whitman Houses in what appears to be a drug deal gone wrong. The identities of the men murdered have not yet been released. Detectives describe the scene as horrific. Eyewitnesses say that several men disguised as DEA agents burst into the apartment to rob the place, tied up the occupants, and then executed them. So far, police have no suspects in custody as their investigation continues."*

For now, it looked like Jamel and his crew had gotten away with murder. The robbery netted them close to a hundred thousand and a few kilos to sell on the streets. Jamel kept the kilos, and his team divided the cash amongst themselves. To them, it was easy money.

Now he had some personal business to attend to.

Jamel slid the hammer to the Glock 19 back and sat patiently in the parked car across the street and observed PJ climb out of his red Lexus and walk into the split-level Queens home. He had no idea that he was being watched. Jamel was ready to strike the man down like a bolt of lightning for disrespecting his family. Ana, short for Anastasia, had called him crying. PJ had beaten her badly. He'd fractured her eye socket and almost killed her. She was the twins' sister, someone Apple and Kola did not know about.

Ana was staying in Queens with PJ, her boyfriend. He was a dangerous drug dealer. He had been abusive to her since their relationship started, just as he'd been with every last one of his past girlfriends. Ana was catching hell from him.

Jamel and Kamel never liked him, but they stayed out of their sister's business. She was a grown woman.

When Jamel saw her face, swollen and bruised, her eye socket fractured, he nearly went insane. He scowled, clenched his fists, and cursed Ana's loyalty to PJ. Jamel *been* wanted to kill him, but because his little sister was so in love with him, he held back his aggression toward the man.

"Please don't kill him," she had begged Jamel. "It wasn't all his fault."

"Look at ya fuckin' face."

Their love and relationship was tainted with acid, but Ana wasn't a peach herself. She had a record for shoplifting, assault, robbery, drug dealing, and credit card fraud. Her angelic features had people fooled. She had temper tantrums, and she had a hard time keeping her hands off someone when she got mad.

Sitting in the shadows, Jamel smoked a cigarette and surveyed the house and the area. He was crazy enough to march up to the house, knock on the door, and blow PJ's brains out where he stood. But Ana was home, and he didn't want her to witness anything like that.

He sat and simply watched the house. PJ's demise was about to come soon.

An hour later Jamel was still waiting, smoking his umpteenth cigarette. Finally, he saw PJ leave the house and get into his Lexus.

Jamel carefully followed the car for miles. He was itching to get at Ana's boyfriend. He had to be careful and do it right. PJ was connected to a violent Blood crew that would quickly retaliate if anything were to happen to him.

Jamel wasn't scared of them, but he had enough people trying to kill him, and he wasn't in any rush to add more names to the list.

PJ exited off the Southern State Parkway and drove through the Baldwin neighborhood in southern Nassau County. Jamel followed him to a ranch-style home on a tree-lined street. He parked in the distance and observed his mark get out of his car and walk to the front door. It opened up, and a petite young blonde came flying out the house and into his arms. It was obvious PJ was fucking this bitch.

The night was growing old, and Jamel didn't want to waste his time on the muthafucka. He was itching to take him out and go get some pussy.

Jamel stepped out of his car and walked toward the house. The block was quiet; it was late, and the house he was watching had turned dark. He leaped over a short white fence and crept into the backyard, his pistol tucked into his waistband. He went toward a window and carefully peeked inside. To some extent he was able to see into one of the bedrooms. Lucky to have picked the right window, he had eyes on PJ having sex with the white girl in the missionary position.

An hour later, PJ exited and climbed back into his Lexus and drove away, and once again Jamel followed him. When they were in a secluded area in Long Island, Jamel purposely tapped into the back of his Lexus.

Like Jamel predicted, PJ came to a sudden stop and jumped out of his ride for a confrontation.

"What the fuck, nigga! You can't fuckin' drive?"

Jamel jumped out too, looking apologetic, his pistol hidden behind his back. He approached PJ with his head down and uttered, "Yo, my bad. I didn't even see you."

PJ was ready to punch Jamel in the face for fucking up his ride.

When Jamel got close to PJ, he aimed the gun at his chest abruptly. PJ stood frozen, wide-eyed with shock. Then he recognized the driver.

"Yo-yo, listen, I-I-I—"

"Yeah, nigga, you fucked wit' the wrong bitch!"

Jamel fired twice, pumping two hot rounds into PJ's chest, propelling him backwards. Jamel watched PJ stumble, fall against his car, and then collapse against the pavement. He was dead.

Jamel glanced around uneasily. There was no one around. He quickly popped the trunk to the Lexus and stuffed PJ's body inside. He climbed back into his car and drove off, leaving the Lexus on the side of the road with the body to rot inside the trunk.

Fuck it! Leave the nigga where he was shot at and let the cops or his crew find him. That bitch-ass nigga deserved to die.

Jamel felt he did it clean and was positive that no one would connect him to the murder. Driving away from the crime scene, he got on his cell phone and called Kamel.

"It's about time I fuckin' heard from you," Kamel said quickly. "Where the fuck have you been? I've been fuckin' calling you!"

"I've been busy, bro."

"We need to meet and talk."

"Yeah, I need to talk to you anyway," Jamel replied. "I'm about to go pick up Ana."

"Ana? Why?"

"That nigga beat on her again, and it was really bad this time. She can't stay there anymore. It's not safe for her there."

"What did you do, Jamel?"

"I didn't do shit! She called me lookin' for help, and she's family, Twin, so I'm gonna help her."

"PJ got a lot of connections, Jamel. You touch him and you know the type of backlash that will bring our way, and to Ana."

"Nigga, I said I ain't touched that nigga. I'm just gonna go pick her up and take her out of there. You should have seen her fuckin' face, nigga. He could have beaten her to death," Jamel proclaimed angrily.

Kamel sighed. "Okay, go pick her up and bring her to Staten Island." "Staten Island?"

"Yes, nigga. If you would fuckin' answer your phone from time to time, then you would know that's where I moved everyone. I'll text you the address and meet you there."

"A'ight, Twin, I'll meet you there." He hung up and sped back to Queens.

FOURTEEN

Jamel hurried back to Queens and knocked on Ana's door. The minute she opened up, he charged inside and said, "Pack ya shit and let's go."

"What! Why?" she asked. "And go fuckin' where?"

"You can't stay here anymore. You comin' wit' me right now."

"Jamel, I can't go. You just can't come into my fuckin' home and force me to leave."

"Yes the fuck I can!"

"I gotta wait for PJ."

"Fuck that nigga! Look what he did to your fuckin' face!" Jamel grabbed her chin roughly and stared intently at her. "How could you let that nigga do this shit to you? Huh? How can you love a clown nigga like that?"

"Because I do!" she spat back.

"Yo, fuck him! We out. I'm not taking no for a fuckin' answer. I got someplace better for you to go."

"Jamel, I ain't fuckin' leaving!" Ana shouted. Her eyes lit up like fire. She was always a hard ass.

Jamel was seething. Her reluctance made him want to knock her down and drag her out to the car by her hair, caveman-style.

"Look, Kamel wants you away from here too. He wants you to stay at his place. He's worried about you, Ana."

Hearing Kamel's name softened her attitude a little bit. She was close with both twins, but Kamel was her favorite. He was always easy to talk to, while sometimes Jamel could be the overbearing big brother always breathing down her neck. There was always something about Kamel that she respected. He could get her to do anything, even leave suddenly from her home.

"Where is he?" she asked.

"You'll find out when you see him."

"He don't come by or talk to me in almost a year, and suddenly I'm supposed to leave my home and my man?"

"Why you always so fuckin' difficult, Ana? Dammit! A nigga tryin' to look out for you and you being a fuckin' bitch right now."

"Fuck you, Jamel!"

"No. Fuck *you!*"

Jamel was one step away from drawing his gun and forcing her into his car and driving off with her kicking and screaming. But he didn't need the unwanted attention from her neighbors.

He thought of another way to handle the situation. Jamel quickly called his brother. He was sure his brother could persuade her; he always could.

Kamel answered after the second ring.

Jamel said, "Yo, you talk to li'l sis about leaving, because she is being fuckin' difficult right now."

Jamel handed Ana the cell phone.

Kamel quickly was in her ear saying, "Ana, I know I've been too busy to come and see you. I'll make it up to you, promise. But listen to Jamel and leave there right now. Anyone connected to us could be in danger."

"What's going on, Kamel?"

"A lot. I'll tell you later. But, baby girl, just trust me and leave with Jamel."

Ana sighed. "Okay, but this better be important. You owe me."

"I know I do. Thanks."

The call ended.

Jamel frowned and said, "You fuckin' happy?"

"Do I look fuckin' happy, dumbass!"

After Ana hurriedly packed a few of her belongings into a small bag, Jamel rushed her out of her home and into his car. She still didn't want to leave, but she wanted to see Kamel again, and what he'd said scared her.

Before Jamel pulled out of her driveway, she asked, "What about PJ?"

"I'm sure he'll pop up soon, so don't worry about him. He's dead to us right now."

Jamel backed out of the driveway and sped away with Ana in the front seat, her arms crossed tightly across her chest. She was silent and pouting. He drove away from Queens via the Belt Parkway.

He looked at Ana and smiled. "You look pretty tonight."

"Fuck off! I'm still mad at you."

He laughed. "Of course, you are, li'l sis."

FIFTEEN

What happened?" Apple asked Kola. "What did he say to you?"
"We just talked and had dinner."

"That's all?" Apple looked at her sister in wonder.

"Yes, there was no threat from him."

"I don't believe it. Y'all just ate and talked? About what?"

"We talked about everything."

"Everything? What the fuck you talkin' about, Kola? You told this nigga all of our damn business?"

"No, I'm not stupid. He just wanted to get to know me—actually, us."

"Well, I don't want to get to know him."

Apple was dumbfounded. She didn't believe Mack D wanted to meet with her sister just to talk. Deep in her heart, she knew he was plotting something. But she was glad that Kola came back home to her safe and sound. While Kola was away risking her life, Apple was extremely worried and concerned. If anything had happened to Kola, Apple wouldn't have stopped until everybody in Mack D's organization was dead.

The two sat in the living room to talk. The kids were in the bedroom sleeping. Apple had covered and lied for her sister. When Kamel called looking for her earlier that afternoon, Apple told him she went to the park with the kids and left her cell phone at the house. He believed her.

"I still can't believe you went to go see him," Apple said.

"I had to."

"You didn't have to do shit. That was a huge risk you took."

"I know, but I learned a couple things."

"Like?"

"Like, until he trusts me there's no way I'm getting near him holding heat. His goons gave me a full pat down."

"You had to expect that."

"I did. My challenge is to get him to allow me in his presence without the security check."

"What else?"

"I learned that he has a massive ego."

"Don't most get-money niggas?"

Kola nodded. "But there's an underlining insecurity attached to him. It's a weakness. I have to make him believe that out of everyone I've known, his accomplishments are the most impressive."

"More than Eduardo?"

"Yup."

"Good luck wit' that." Apple chuckled.

Kola began giggling as well, and then got serious. "I don't think I did a good job today earning his trust."

"Why you feel that?"

"Just a gut feeling. There were so many emotions I had to process, but I have to just stay focused, despite my true feelings for him."

"Promise me that you won't make a move on this nigga, any move, without consulting with me first."

"No doubt."

"Kola, seriously. We always have been smart, and we got each other now. We work better together than against each other."

Kola took this opportunity to go and retrieve the coats from out of her room. She came back inside the living room and tossed both coats at Apple's feet. A huge grin spread across Apple's face. Immediately she reached for the red one.

"This me?" Apple tried on the mink coat and ran her fingers over the soft, natural fibers. "I like the purple one too, though."

Kola smiled. "Well, I didn't buy them."

"Who then? Jamel? Kamel?"

Kola shook her head and Apple finally caught on.

"I don't want anything from him, Kola!" Apple removed the coat and flung it across the room. "Can't you see what he's trying to do?"

"I do, Apple. I'm not stupid. I know this coat comes with strings attached, but we have to play the game."

"No *we don't.*"

"Well, I do. I have to keep our enemies close. Trust me. I know what I'm doing. This all plays out one way, and that's with Mack D dead. Either now or the near future."

"So why can't we just kill that muthafucka? Why this game?"

"You know it's not that easy, Apple. Mack D ain't some block-hugging thug."

"And we ain't block-hugging bitches. We can do this. You and I, together. Us."

"We can't because we finally have someone to live for. We have to do things right because we have three kids that love and need us, alive. We can't take any chances. Not one. And I have to make you see that, Apple. We're parents now. That means something."

Apple lit a cigarette and took a few drags. She looked at her sister with a kind stare and said, "I like this, Kola—what we got going between us. I missed this, and I don't want this to end."

"I don't want it to end either, Apple."

"I will always have your back."

"Same here," Kola replied.

Apple smiled at Kola. She melted Apple with a grin that took her back to when they were kids. Though Apple was forty-six minutes older, Kola was somewhat her teenage idol in many ways growing up. Kola did everything first, cutting her own path and making her own way. She didn't need to depend on anyone or listen to anyone, especially Denise. Kola accomplished a lot at an early age, thrusting herself into the street life and becoming the first lady of a fierce drug crew in their area.

Kola envied her sister in some ways. Apple had a child, and she didn't. Apple didn't know that the gynecologist had informed Kola years ago that it would be difficult to have children due to scarring in her fallopian tubes caused by an untreated STD. Her wild lifestyle had caught up to her.

She kept it a secret from everyone she had fallen in love with, always hoping that she would conceive. It was a painful and haunting feeling. So she grew to love Peaches and the siblings greatly. Where she once felt a huge void, the children had filled it sevenfold. They were a beautiful distraction from her unbearable issues.

Kola felt that she needed to protect Apple from Apple. If she didn't, Apple would become a victim to the inevitable—her own self-destruction. Apple was a mother now, but she still had some kinks inside of her.

Kamel stepped into the living room and looked at the sisters bonding. He had his cell phone in his hand and looked upset about something.

Kola looked his way and asked, "Is everything okay, baby?"

"Yeah, everything's cool. Jamel's on his way over."

"He is?" Apple perked up. "Is he okay?"

"Yeah, he's cool."

Kola on the other hand, looked cheerless about the news. She didn't want to see Jamel, not after he tricked her into having sex with him. She wished he stayed where he was at.

Jamel pulled into the driveway. Ana was in the passenger seat and still frowning. It had been a quiet drive from Queens to the bottom of Staten Island. Both of them looked at the Staten Island home like they'd just swallowed a sour lemon. It was quaint, to say the least.

"This is it?" Ana fussed.

"Kamel said to bring you here."

Ana sighed with irritation. Ana was a five-star bitch. From clothes to shoes, she didn't accept anything but the best. She didn't want to be there, preferring to wait around for PJ. However, she was also excited to see Kamel again.

Jamel climbed out of the car, and Ana followed.

Right on cue, Kamel came walking out of the front door and glared at Jamel. He wanted to put his fist through his brother's face. How could he be so ignorant? But then his frown changed into a smile when he set his eyes on Ana.

Jamel walked around the car to his brother looking stoic.

Ana smiled. Her face still showed violent signs of abuse, but behind the mask of mistreatment, she was a beautiful woman. She stood five seven with dark, shoulder-length hair, and caramel skin. Ana was a young, vibrant twenty-year-old.

Apple and Kola walked outside to see who had pulled up in the driveway. Apple uttered, "Who the fuck is this bitch!"

Kola arched her eyebrow as she watched Kamel hug the young girl with a wide smile.

The twins stepped off the porch, both ready for a confrontation if it came down to it.

"Who is she?" Apple asked abrasively, frowning.

Jamel stepped between Ana and the twins and said, "She's our baby sister."

"Baby sister?" Apple and Kola said simultaneously.

Ana looked at the twins with a steely glare. She was quiet. Even with her face beaten, she still stood with assertiveness and cockiness.

"Why didn't you tell us that y'all had a sister?" Kola asked.

"I'm telling you now. Anyway, she's staying with us because she needed to get out of Queens. She needs our protection," Jamel stated.

"Protection from who or what?" Apple asked.

Jamel didn't bother to answer her question. He said to Ana, "I'll show you inside," like it was his place and he had been staying there. He walked away from Apple and Kola, leaving Apple hanging on dumbfounded by his bold action and shooting Kamel a curt look.

"This muthafucka!" Apple uttered with contempt.

Everyone turned in their direction and followed behind Jamel inside the residence.

Jamel looked around and said, "It's decent. Not your usual style, Kamel, but it's cool."

"We need to talk," Kamel said to his brother in a gruff voice.

"I know."

Kamel stood near his brother like a savage dog ready to pounce on an unwanted intruder, his eyes burning into his brother's flesh.

Jamel smiled at Ana and said, "You good here. Get to know the girls. Me and bro gotta talk 'bout something for a moment."

Jamel and Kamel went down into the small, dank basement to talk privately, leaving Ana alone with the twin sisters.

"So you their little sister, huh? Why they never mentioned you before?" Apple asked. "Why come around now?"

"I don't know. Ask them," Ana said with a sharp attitude. "And who are y'all?"

"I'm Jamel's girlfriend," Apple quickly let known.

"My brother doesn't have girlfriends," Ana said with a prickly smirk.

"Well he has one now, bitch!" Apple snapped.

Ana waved her hand in the air dismissively and replied, "Cute."

Instantly, Kola didn't like this bitch and didn't want any parts of the entire arrangement. There was something about Ana that immediately rubbed her the wrong way.

"Don't think your brothers will save you and your slick ass mouth, because you will get beat the fuck up in here." Apple stepped closer invading Ana's space. "You already look like you on the losing end of someone's fist. Trust, you don't want to go a couple rounds wit' me."

Ana looked past Apple to Kola and asked, "So where do I stay? It ain't like I wanna be here anyway."

Ana was under the impression that the sisters were supposed to kiss her ass, like the past girlfriends of her brothers.

"I'll show you where you're gonna sleep," was the only thing Kola said to her.

The small three-bedroom house was bursting at the seams. How could it hold seven, possibly eight people? Kola hoped that this beef would blow over soon so she could go back to the downtown Manhattan condo with all its amenities.

Ana followed behind Kola, while Apple stood in the hallway, brooding. Any other bitch would have gotten her teeth knocked out.

Once they were alone in the basement, Kamel shocked his brother with a right hook to the side of his face, and Jamel went flying backwards. Before Jamel could get his footing, Kamel was on him like white on rice. Kamel grabbed him by his collar and slammed him into the wall, shouting, "What the fuck is wrong with you? What the fuck did you do?"

"Yo, nigga, get ya fuckin' hands off me! You crazy, nigga!" Scowling, Jamel quickly pushed Kamel off him.

"I told you PJ was connected!"

"I ain't do shit, nigga! It wasn't me!"

"Nigga, don't fuckin' lie to me. The streets are lit up. State Troopers found his body in the trunk of his car still warm."

"I told you it wasn't me. I had nothing to do wit' that shit. I just went and picked up Ana, and he was already gone when I got there," Jamel stated almost convincingly.

Kamel was fuming. His fists clenched, he continued glaring at his brother. Kamel found it hard to believe, knowing his brother's violent and murderous reputation.

Jamel rubbed the side of his face, soothing his jaw. He was okay. He gave his brother a pass for the sucker punch. Anyone else would have immediately seen the end of his gun barrel.

"What happened in Queens?" Kamel asked.

"I don't know. It ain't like that nigga was a fuckin' saint, Kamel. PJ was an asshole, and he had enemies. Fuck him! I'm glad he's dead. Look what he did to Ana's face. But I didn't do it. I never saw the nigga."

Kamel didn't know what to believe. He started to pace back and forth in front of Jamel. No matter what he believed, Kamel had sense enough to know that PJ's death was about to blow back on them. It was a good thing he got his family out of Brooklyn; his next step was moving them out of state until things cooled over.

"Look, you need to calm the fuck down in these streets and fuckin' think before you react," Kamel said.

"I do think, nigga. I'm thinkin' about our future and surviving out there while you in here tryin' to play fuckin' house."

Kamel tightened his face and stepped closer to his brother. If he said anything disrespectful about Kola, he was going to hit him again. No one was going to say or do anything foul to his woman.

"You just don't get it, nigga. You never will," Kamel said.

Jamel chuckled like he didn't give a fuck what his brother said. He was in the streets making a name for himself, trying to make money.

"Look, I gotta go. I got things to do. We finished here?" Jamel asked.

"Yeah, we finished."

"I love you too, bro." As Jamel walked away, he purposely bumped into his brother and left the basement.

Kamel stood there for a moment and thought about the consequences of his brother's actions and thought, *what now?*

SIXTEEN

Mack D sat back comfortably in his eighty-thousand-dollar truck and checked stocks on his cell phone as Richard navigated the vehicle through the crowded Brooklyn streets. He gazed out the window as he rode through Brownsville, one of the poorer neighborhoods in the city. Crime and poverty was rampant, the streets were inundated with many of the unfortunate—the homeless, the drug addicts, the unemployed, the desperate, and the broke dreamers. The bodegas and shops were dilapidated. The project buildings that housed the low income were the only thing soaring in the neighborhood.

One of his investments was down thirty-five percent. Losing money always bothered Mack D. He played to win, from Wall Street to the real streets. He wanted to be a master of both book knowledge and street knowledge. Once you mastered both worlds, then you were untouchable.

When Mack D saw the latest report coming in from Wall Street, he cringed. The thirty-five percent he lost was a quarter of a million dollars. He quickly jumped on the phone to curse out his broker.

He took a few pulls from his cigar and said into the phone, "I hate to lose, Cornell. I need you to fully understand that. Fix it before I fix you."

If one of Mack D's workers had lost that much money in the streets, they would have been dead. Though this was legit business, he still wanted to put a bullet in his broker's head.

"Business is a muthafucka, Richard. It's like being in the fuckin' jungle. The predators feed on the weak. These companies want to devour everything until there's nothing left."

Richard nodded, listening and driving. He couldn't understand why his boss was so angry with the broker. He couldn't fix the stock market. It doesn't work like that. The market fluctuates; people lose, people win. If you can't absorb both, then you're in the wrong game.

Richard knew Mack D was in over his head. He spewed lines he would hear on television to his underlings who were impressionable. The only thing that impressed Richard was laying a nigga flat on his back, moving tons of kilos, and fucking unlimited bitches with wet pussies.

Mack D continued to ramble on. "Look at this shit out here—Muthafuckas living like zero, struggling for scraps. There's no end game for them. You know why? Because these niggas can't play the game. They don't know how; they never learned. This is chess, where every move you make needs to matter, or else it will cost you the game."

Richard continued to listen, driving north on Rockaway Avenue.

Mack D went on to quote several lines from one of his favorite movies, *Wall Street as if they were his own.*

Richard sarcastically asked, "Have you ever seen the movie Wall Street?"

"What, muthafucka?"

"Nevermind."

Richard came to a stop in front of an old-fashioned meat market on Sutter Avenue. Richard and Mack D climbed out of the truck and walked inside.

The young goon standing guard at the front door expected Mack D's arrival. He opened the door for him. Mack D nodded and entered the dim shop.

"Downstairs," he told Mack D.

Mack D nodded and slipped him a hundred-dollar bill.

"Appreciate it," the man replied.

It was nothing. Mack D appreciated loyalty. He and Richard descended into the concrete basement. They went into the large meat fridge, where slabs of butchered meat were hung up and displayed, and a half-dozen men were gathered around something. When they saw Mack D, they parted like the Red Sea and allowed him to pass.

Mack D glared at a naked man who had been badly beaten and tied to a large meat table with rope. Facing up and whimpering, his arms and legs were stretched to the limit.

When he saw Mack D, his eyes opened up with tremendous fear.

"I swear, Lowell and Mogen are worth every damn penny," Mack D said out loud about the two detectives on his payroll.

The man cried out, "Mack D, I swear to you, I didn't have anything to do with stealing from you. It wasn't me!"

"It wasn't you, huh? So you weren't part of taking close to a quarter of a million dollars of my money? So tell me, Zink—why disappear for two weeks?"

"My mother was sick. I had to go check on her," he quickly explained.

"A sick mother." Mack D laughed. "Such a cliché."

"Mack D, I'm serious. She has cancer. She's dying."

"I want to believe you, Zink, but here's the problem—I don't." Mack D stood over Zink with a terrifying gaze that could make a lion cower.

Zink shivered tremendously in the meat locker.

"You see, Zink, I like my money, and I care for it. But it isn't just about you boldly taking what belongs to me, but the principle—You're a fuckin' thief, and I hate thieves!

"Now, I'm gonna give you a choice. Tell me where I can find your two friends and my money, and I promise, I'll make this just about you and not your family. I'll make this go very quick for you, Zink."

Zink cried, "C'mon, I didn't do it. I'm not a fuckin' thief."

"Okay, you're still sticking with that story. It's your choice." Mack D nodded to one of his men, named Chopper.

Without hesitation Chopper took a large butcher knife and chopped off Zink's right pinky finger.

Zink screamed out in extreme pain.

"Talk to me. Where are they?"

"I don't know. On everything I love, I'm telling you the truth!"

Mack D nodded again, and Chopper removed the right thumb, which took more effort.

"Aaaaaaaaahhhh, make him stop! Please! Please!" he hollered crazily, squirming violently against his restraints.

Mack D nodded, and Chopper stopped.

"Talk to me. Where are they?"

"I don't know. I swear to you," Zink replied in a shaky tone.

Mack D gave a stern stare to Chopper, and he began to slowly remove the remaining fingers from Zink's right hand.

Zink's agonizing screams echoed throughout the meat fridge, but there would be no help. The other men watched the torture without flinching. They were all hardcore killers in their own right, so it was easy for them to watch a man be dismembered.

Mack D fixated his eyes on Zink.

"Where's your accomplices? And where's my money? Talk, muthafucka, talk!"

Zink's eyes were searching around the room as if he were trying to come up with a really good story. He was desperate.

"I can find them—if you allow me to leave then I'll find them and kill them myself for you, boss!"

"How you gonna kill someone, young blood, when you can't hold a gat?"

Mack D nodded, and Chopper started on Zink's left hand. All his fingers were removed. "He'll talk."

There was more screaming.

"Last chance. Tell me what I want to fuckin' know!"

Zink began to whimper. He knew three things to be true. He did help rob Mack D for the money, his mother did have cancer, and regardless of what he said or did, he was going to die in that room.

"Yo, Mack, you ain't gotta do this, man. It's only money. I can work it off—"

Bak, bak!

Mack D pulled out his pistol and shot two bullets into his head for speaking to him as if he were petty. Zink lay lifeless against the meat table.

Mack D was upset. He still didn't have the information he wanted. He scowled down at the body, hating that Zink had died so fast. He'd wanted the torture to last a long time.

"Get rid of this muthafucka." He turned and started to leave, but before he made his exit, he turned with an afterthought. "In fact, make a public display of the nigga. Dump his body in public and let niggas know this is what happens to niggas who steal from me."

His men nodded.

Mack D left the room with Richard right behind him. They walked out of the meat shop and got back into the SUV.

Before they drove off, Mack D lit another cigar. "One down, two to go."

He got on his cell phone and texted Kola: *I want to see you. Call me.*

He then proclaimed, "If your enemy is superior, evade him. If angry, irritate him. If equally matched, fight, and if not, split and re-evaluate."

Richard sat in silence, confused by Mack D's words.

"It was just some shit I heard from a nigga in prison," Mack D explained. "Take me home."

SEVENTEEN

S team filled the room as Ana took a lengthy shower and enjoyed the water cascading down on her naked body. She bathed her skin lightly, taking care not to touch the bruises that dotted her body. She was healing well. The water poured down, dripping by her sides, as everything became a foggy illusion.

Ana sighed heavily, thinking and wondering. The sensation of the steamy water calmed her a little bit, but it didn't take her mind completely off her troubles. When she found out PJ was found dead in the trunk of his car, she went berserk and burst out into tears.

Jamel and Kamel were there to calm her down.

Apple and Kola watched from the sidelines. They understood how it felt to lose a loved one, but they weren't so quick to console her.

Who killed PJ? Why did it happen? Why was it so urgent for her to leave her home so suddenly? Was it because of the murder? What mess were Jamel and Kamel in now?

Questions, questions, there were so many of them, and no one was saying anything to her. So to pass the time, Ana indulged herself by drinking bottles of Hennessy straight up. Still, she barely slept.

As Ana wallowed in her grief trying to dull the pain with alcohol, Apple started to soften up to her. She asked her what happened, meaning the bruises. Ana didn't want to get into details. She didn't like spilling her life out to strangers, but there was something about Apple that she felt she could connect to.

"PJ. It was him. He had a hand problem, but not nothing I couldn't handle."

"Y'all fought a lot?"

"Yeah, that nigga was always tripping, but he loved the ground I walked on."

Apple thought about Supreme. "That fighting shit was really to control you, keep your ass locked up in the house hiding your bruises."

"You speaking from experience?" Ana asked, knowing her brother wasn't an angel.

"I wish a nigga would beat my ass and I just sit there looking helpless—" Apple rolled her eyes. "I mean no disrespect."

"None taken. And for the record, I never just sat there. I go for mines too. He got his battle scars from me."

Apple was still trying to feel her out.

Kola, however, was a different story. She didn't know Ana, and she didn't want to get to know her. She considered all of this only temporary.

Apple and Ana started smoking weed together, and, as a result, the two bonded. When Kola came in one day—house filled with fumes, she was heated. She pushed opened the bedroom door and saw Apple and Ana sitting on the floor giggling like schoolgirls.

"What the fuck y'all doing?" Kola screamed.

Calmly, Apple replied, "What it look like?"

"Don't get cute, Apple. Why the fuck y'all lighting up in the house with the kids in the other room? *Your k*id, Apple. In case you forgot."

"She fine, Kola. Damn. A little bit of smoke ain't gonna hurt her. Denise used to light up around us and we didn't lose any brain cells."

"You're using Denise's mothering skills as a blueprint? Really, bitch!"

Ana placed her hands over her ears. "My head . . . I can't . . . please, just stop talking."

Her attempt at humor irritated Kola, who lunged forward and started swinging. She got a couple of headshots on Ana before Apple quickly broke it up.

"Get off me, Apple," Kola screamed. "I'ma hurt this bitch!"

Kola couldn't help but notice that Apple had grabbed her extra tight. She also couldn't help but notice that instead of Apple spending her free time with her and the kids, she and Ana became inseparable overnight.

Kola backed off. "Take that shit outside!"

Ana and Apple did just that. They both climbed into the back seat of Kamel's Lexus. The lifted feeling they had felt prior to Kola raining on their parade was gone. They had to start over.

"You wanna get high?" Ana asked Apple.

"Bitch what we been doing?"

Ana pulled out a pre-rolled blunt and held it up to Apple. "Nah, we were getting nice. This blunt right here will get us high. Maybe higher than you've ever been."

Apple sucked her teeth. "Bitch, light up."

"Don't say I didn't warn you."

"Warn me? This ain't crack, right?"

Ana chuckled. "Do I look like a low-grade crack bitch?"

Ana flicked her Bic several times before the blunt glowed hues of deep orange and yellow. She placed her small, pouty lips on the blunt and inhaled deeply before passing it off to Apple.

Apple repeated the movement. As soon as the blunt began to infiltrate Apple's body, she felt invincible. Some potent shit raced through her body, and it blew her mind. Her heart sped up, palpitating at a faster rate before suddenly slowing down and evening out. She mellowed into a blissful state that was indescribable. From Ana's one blunt she felt higher than she did after smoking ten of her own blunts.

"This is some bomb weed," Apple complimented. "Did you get it from Jamel? I only get this high when I smoke his shit."

"Nah, this my shit. We both lace our blunts with cocaine."

Apple wanted to react, but she was too high. One part of her wanted to fuck Ana up. The other part—the much more prominent side—was just grateful to be feeling this good.

"You know what? I like you, Ana. You got a lot of balls giving me some tainted shit," Apple said, high out of her mind. "I ain't no fiend. I don't use cocaine; I sell it by the kilo."

"I ain't no fiend either," Ana said. "This ain't some low-level dime bag of crack. This is some high end, expensive shit. Only exclusive bitches can handle this right here."

An hour later the two stumbled back into the house to Kola's dismay. If looks could kill Ana would have been dead. Catching the shade, Ana hurried off to the bedroom. When Apple tried to follow, Kola grabbed her sternly by her forearm.

"We gotta talk."

"Not now, Kola. Please." Apple's eyes were low, and her mouth was extremely dry.

"I don't like what's going on here, Apple. You're clinging to Ana like you're her shadow."

"It ain't even like that. She's the twins' sister."

"Yes, she's their sister; not yours! I'm your sister, Apple. And next time I swing on a bitch you better swing too!"

Kola walked away and slammed her bedroom door.

Ana, who was ear hustling from the other room had heard it all. She quickly ran from the door.

When Apple came in she asked, "Wanna go par-tay tonight?"

EIGHTEEN

Ana and Apple got dressed in their skimpy club outfits and went out to paint the town red—Partying for Ana was another way of coping with her loss.

"What's up wit' that coat?" Ana asked. She had been salivating over that red mink since she first laid eyes on it. "Could I wear it if you're not?"

"Nah, that's not a good idea."

Apple didn't feel compelled to give Ana an explanation. She didn't want that coat worn by anyone. Once Mack D was dead, Ana could have it. It meant nothing to her.

"Okay—um, cool. I'm still a pretty bitch."

Apple smiled. "You look a'ight."

Ana threw on a pair of dark sunglasses and lipstick to help hide her bruises—new and old. The dim club lights also helped. They hit two nightclubs in the city and drank heavily. They flirted with the men and tore up the dance floor together. The men were almost knocking each other over to buy them their choice of drinks.

They got home an hour before the sun rose. Both girls passed out in the living room. Ana was sprawled out on the couch, and Apple was lying face down on the carpet.

⬥

Kola was highly upset. She felt they were setting a bad example to the children. Apple especially wasn't being a mother to her daughter. Kola took on Apple's responsibilities and shielded Peaches from her mother's reckless ways.

And then there was Ana. A lazy, messy bitch. The sink was filled with her dirty dishes, her clothes were everywhere, and she constantly left her wet towels on the bathroom floor. Kola watched Ana with suspicious eyes. She didn't like the way Ana flaunted herself in front of the brothers when they were home, wearing the tightest shorts and smallest tops, especially around Kamel. It was just weird. Kola wasn't shy in telling the bitch off. She wasn't about to kiss her ass because she was Kamel's little sister.

"You need to clean up after yourself. I ain't no maid."

Ana sucked her teeth. "I'll do it later," she replied nonchalantly. "You seen Apple?"

"Don't think I'm stupid. I know what you and her been doing. It needs to fuckin' stop."

Ana frowned. "Doing what?"

"Bitch, don't fuckin' play stupid with me. My sister was doing fine until you came around. And now she's out there acting a fool with you."

"Apple's a grown woman, Kola. Why you all in your sister's business?"

"Why are you all up her ass!"

"You jealous cause no one's up yours!"

"Watch your mouth, little girl."

Ana sucked her teeth and rolled her eyes. "Ain't no little girl around here, so don't get shit twisted. Bitch!"

Ana pivoted and walked away feeling like she'd won the standoff.

Kola kept her composure and didn't go running after Ana. She knew that if Ana kept popping off at the mouth that she was going to put a serious hurting on her. But not in front of the kids.

Kola went into her bedroom, and the minute she closed her door, she received the text from Mack D asking to see her again. She stared at the text and was skeptical for a moment, but then she texted him back: *When and where? I'm available.*

She took a deep breath. She had bigger things to worry about than Ana.

Kola climbed into the Maybach S600 on the corner of Lafayette and Canal Street, but not before getting patted down by the driver. She quickly went from the yellow cab into luxuriousness, and was shocked to see Mack D seated in the backseat this time, smoking his cigar, watching the stock market report on the small flat-screen embedded in the back of the headrest.

Mack D, dressed like he was about to attend the Grammy awards in Hollywood, greeted Kola with a brief smile and said, "Let's go for a ride and talk."

As the driver merged into the city traffic, Kola sat back and brooded for a moment. She trusted Apple to watch the kids, but she didn't trust Ana inside her home.

It was twilight. Like always, Manhattan was alive, busy and constantly moving like a well-oiled machine. Lights shone everywhere like stars in the midnight sky, and buildings towered above everyone.

"I'm glad you came," Mack D said.

"I wasn't at first," she said.

"What changed your mind?"

"I just needed to get out of the house."

"Problems?"

Kola didn't say anything to him at first. She sighed, thinking about how things had changed so suddenly last week. Ana's arrival made everything topsy-turvy.

"Nothing that I can't handle," she replied.

"Well, you know I'm always here to help."

She nodded and gazed out the window, her eyes on the everyday people. The sidewalks were crowded with people of every ethnicity, and there were yellow cabs and traffic headed in every direction. Lower Manhattan was like a clogged artery, congested and looking like it was about to have a heart attack.

The driver headed east, toward the FDR.

"Where are we going?"

"Are you hungry?"

"A little."

"Then we'll get something to eat. I know a nice place. Nice food, nice wine."

Kola didn't mind munching on a good meal. She could use a drink and some time away from everything.

Once again, she had to lie about her whereabouts to Kamel. While he had his hands full with the streets, it gave her room to meet with Mack D behind his back. It almost felt like Kola was having an affair with her sneaking around, though that was far from the case. .

"You know you can talk to me about anything," Mack D said.

"I appreciate that. Thank you."

"So what's on your mind?"

"Just family," she answered.

"Family, huh? Is it Apple?" Mack D gazed at her, pulling on his cigar.

There was a short moment of silence. It looked like Kola was ready to burst with a fiery response.

"She's just so stupid," Kola said, upset.

"What is she doing?"

"She isn't doing what she supposed to be doing."

Mack D looked at the stock report momentarily and then glanced out the window.

There was more silence inside the car.

"You look beautiful, by the way," he said out of the blue.

"Thank you. And you look handsome."

"Tonight, I'll get your mind away from your worries, and make up for the lost time with my daughter," he said.

Kola didn't correct him this time. If he wanted to make up being absent from Nichols' life by treating her nicely, then she planned on benefiting from it. It was all part of her plan.

Fifteen minutes later, the Maybach came to a stop in front of a midtown restaurant called Annisa. The driver stepped out and opened the passenger door for Mack D and Kola to get out. The sleek vehicle turned heads, and Mack D and Kola looked like a celebrity couple; the only thing missing were the paparazzi.

Annisa wasn't the kind of place where you could get a table on impulse—reservations were required. Inside, there were large windows, long embroidered curtains, and the smell of fresh bread and soup permeated the air. White tablecloths, candles, and flowers adorned each table, and delicate live piano music graced the ambiance.

Walking in, Mack D greeted the stiff maitre d' with a nod, and he quickly escorted them to their table. Once they were seated, Kola perused the extensive wine list, occasionally looking around the busy tables. An elderly couple was eating side by side, one glass of wine each, studiously bent over their meals. A group of young women in their thirties were collapsing with giggles as a stern woman dining alone nearby looked on and frowned. A married couple was toasting their happiness together, and there were a few businessmen in dark suits talking business and politics.

"Lovely place," Kola commented after Mack D placed the wine order.

"I come here regularly. I like the food."

A bottle of wine was placed on their table. The really good and expensive stuff. The waiter came to take their orders with a mini tablet computer. As they spoke out their selections, he deftly tapped the screen to transmit their orders straight to the kitchen.

When he walked away, Mack D picked up his wine glass and lifted it toward Kola. "I'd like to propose a toast," he said.

Kola picked up her glass and raised it. "A toast to what?"

"To us. New beginnings. A family reunion. Allah the Father has shown me the way. So take care of the things that He has granted you and be kind to your family and friends. Take care of the environment and don't waste His blessings, such as water and wealth. Also follow His commandments to worship Him as He ordained."

It wasn't an impressive toast, but she went along with it. They clinked glasses and he uttered, "To Allah the Father, and us," which made Kola uncomfortable.

"Have you ever thought about converting, Kola?"

"Never gave it a thought." Kola didn't care for religion. She felt it was hypocritical, preaching one thing but practicing another. It was his belief, not hers. However, she wasn't going to clown him again. She could see that his religion meant a lot to him, and if her goal was to get on his good side then she needed to indulge him.

"While I was inside, I had someone show me the way, and I'm grateful I was smart enough to follow that direction. What I have today—the money, the respect, the knowledge—it is all because of Him."

"And that's what I admire most about you."

Mack D raised his eyebrow. "Really?"

"Yeah, don't be so surprised. You built an empire, brick by brick. How many niggas can say the same?"

"You've had a few."

"But no one has made the transformation you've made. Allah the Father and his teachings helped mold, I guess, who you were always meant to be. Niggas respect and fear you."

"They should."

Mack D went on to tell Kola about his stint in prison, confiding in her about some things he'd never told anybody, including almost being raped. She was shocked to hear such news.

"It was a lesson. I grew and became stronger," he said.

"Almost being raped in prison sounds like a hard lesson. I'll pass."

"When you're older you'll realize that to be afflicted is a blessing. I was honored that I found wisdom in the white devils' prison system."

This wasn't Kola's scene. His ramblings were making her uncomfortable. Any minute she thought he would start saying he saw dead people.

She changed the subject. "This wine is delicious."

He nodded.

"You know, you remind me of her . . . your mother," Mack D said.

"How?"

"You have her attitude and her looks. Feisty and smart, but beautiful. I do miss her."

"I miss her too."

The two continued talking through dinner. The conversation never stopped.

Kola talked about Kamel. When she spoke about him to Mack D, her love and passion for him showed completely. There was no hiding the fact that she was in love. Mack D could see it in her eyes and hear it in her voice.

"He's my everything," she stated.

"No one should ever be your everything," Mack D replied.

"You know what I mean."

"I know what you said. If you love him just say you love him."

Mack D's demeanor changed on a dime. He went from light to dark too quickly.

Kola kept cool. "Yes, I love him."

"And how does Eduardo feel about this?"

Hearing his name brought a cold chill through her body. It was hard for her to try and forget his threats, because he had the ability to strike when she least expected. She didn't want to speak about him.

"I haven't talked to him in a minute," she said.

"Why not?"

"It's personal."

"I see," he said. "Another touchy area with you."

"Very touchy," she said, being honest.

Mack D took a sip of wine and didn't pursue the conversation.

After dinner, they climbed back into the backseat of the Maybach and went for a drive around the city.

Mack D continued talking, spilling his knowledge to her. They started connecting awkwardly. He poured her champagne into a short-stemmed glass, and she relaxed and enjoyed the ride through Manhattan.

As they traveled northbound on Broadway, Mack D pointed to a high-rise building and said, "You see that building? I bought that building seven years ago. It was my first real estate deal when I came home from prison. I sold it three years later, made a profit of two point six million. It was better than sex—making money."

Kola gawked at the building. It was a beautiful piece of property. It had to cost hundreds of millions, and there was no way was he worth that much. Especially not right after prison. He was talking as if he was as big as Eduardo, the head of a huge drug cartel, which he wasn't. Kola began to suspect that Mack D embellished a lot of his accomplishments.

"You have to always think big, Kola. Being comfortable isn't worth it. Getting rich, even if you have to play with rules and be a little merciless, is worth it."

"See, this is what I want . . . to build an empire."

"Didn't you build with Eduardo?"

Kola shook her head. "Once we got together he never allowed me to help him with his business. He thought my place was in his bedroom."

"And you wanted more?"

"Of course I did. I know what I can do. But I wasn't given the opportunity."

"Well, maybe you and I could build together."

"Me? You don't need me."

"I don't need anyone, but I could use a shareholder to help expand my brand."

"What about Richard?"

"He's the muscle. When you wear the crown you have to know how to delegate tasks. With your track record, and your entrepreneurial skills, we could be quite a team. Who knows, Kola? All this could be yours one day."

Mack D and Kola were chauffeured around New York City for the next hour. The champagne kept the conversation flowing.

It seemed like Mack D was becoming the father figure she'd never had. It didn't bother her how their relationship started out; the only thing that mattered to her was how it ended. It seemed like the risk to meet with him was paying off.

NINETEEN

idtown Manhattan was illuminated with lights and teeming with activity. Limousines and luxury vehicles lined the one-way street, while clubgoers jumped out of yellow taxicabs left and right. Apple and Ana climbed out of their cab, laughing like schoolgirls, and strutted toward Club Mayhem's entrance looking like two divas.

The line to get inside was long, and the girls weren't on the list. Apple slipped the bouncer a few hundred dollars. Suddenly the velvet rope was unhooked, and security stepped aside, allowing them to slip inside.

The music was as loud as thunder, and it made the floor rattle. The dance floor was jam-packed, neon lights flashing everywhere. The party was madness.

Rich Homie Quan's "Flex" song got louder, instantly pulling Ana and Apple in. They had no choice but to join the crowd.

Apple and Ana started dancing, their attention on the music. Apple gyrated her bottom suggestively, and Ana winded backwards. They were ready to have a good time and get high and drunk. Apple twerked and Ana followed.

From song to song, they had the stage and were the center of attention. The men were in awe, caught off guard by their strong sexuality.

So many eyes watched them. Even the DJ shouted them out, saying into the mic, "I see two ladies definitely getting it in out there."

"Party over here!" Ana shouted.

It didn't take long before they were approached.

"Let me buy y'all ladies a drink," a man said to them. He was tall and handsome, his eyes dark like onyx.

"You know we don't come cheap, right?" Apple said with a flirtatious smile.

"I like nothing but the best, from my wine to my women. That's why I want y'all to come join me in VIP."

They chuckled.

"I think I already like you," Ana chimed.

The girls followed the dark-skinned man with his curly dark hair toward the VIP area, where his friends were partying. Apple and Ana sat with him and a few of his friends in a U-shaped section, bottles of champagne and liquor right in front of them.

Apple and Ana immediately started downing drinks.

Apple crossed her legs and sat back. She felt the man's arm around her, indicating he really wanted to get to know her. She didn't mind. He was cute.

"What's y'all names?"

"What's your name?" Ana asked him.

He smiled and said, "Tony."

"Well, Tony, I'm Ana, and that's my new friend, Apple."

"How long y'all known each other?

"Since last week," Ana admitted.

"Oh, so y'all just met each other, huh?"

"Uh-huh, like we just meeting you."

"One big happy family, I see," Tony said. "Well, let's all be friends then. Let the good times begin."

Tony got up and pulled out another bottle of Moët from the clear plastic oval ice bucket and popped it open. It spilled lightly, like a volcano erupting, and he started to fill everyone's glasses. His diamond Rolex peeked from underneath the sleeve of his shirt, matching the gleam from his diamond pinky ring.

"It's a party tonight, right?" he exclaimed.

"Hells yeah!" everyone yelled collectively.

Tony plopped down next to Apple. He squeezed himself against her, placing his arm around her shoulder yet again, and stared down at her long, defined legs.

Ana was fine herself, and he and his friends were yearning to take them back to their hotel rooms for some extra fun.

The night continued with the DJ playing his blaring club music like a concert at Madison Square Garden. The neon lights bounced off the walls, and everyone inside partied hard with no signs of slowing down anytime soon. Club Mayhem was turned up.

"You know what this party needs?" Ana said, leaning in.

"What does it need, baby?" Tony asked, a lecherous smile aimed at her.

"Some nose candy. You got some?"

Apple was taken aback by Ana's bold request. Getting blunted with weed laced with coke was one thing in the comfort of your own home, but this was insane.

Tony smiled. He knew exactly what she was talking about. "Baby, you're definitely talking to the right man, because I never leave home without it."

Ana grinned. "Ooooh, I knew I liked you for a reason."

Tony tossed a head nod in his friend's direction. "Hook 'em up."

He nodded back. He stood up and suggested that the girls follow him.

Ana and Apple didn't hesitate, their high heels hurriedly click-clacking against the hard floor and away from the VIP section. They moved through the thick crowd toward the bathroom area.

Tony's friend covertly put a small bag of cocaine into the palm of Ana's hand, and she smiled like an emoji.

"How much?" she asked.

"For now, it's on the house, because y'all cool peoples. Enjoy." He slipped away from them and disappeared into the crowd, leaving the girls to enjoy their treat.

Apple and Ana went into the ladies' bathroom. A few girls were standing by the large, long lit mirror checking their makeup and fixing their hair, chattering and admiring their reflections.

Ana and Apple went into an empty stall farthest from the door and everyone else. Apple pulled out the weed and blunt paper, while Ana pulled out her small compact mirror and sprinkled a little cocaine onto it.

"What are you doing?"

"I'm doing me. You want to hit this?" Ana rolled up a twenty-dollar bill into a straw and started to sniff short lines. It was good shit!

"Don't tell me you're a fuckin' junkie!" Apple eyes were searching Ana's to see any signs of addiction. "I thought we were going to light up and get a couple pulls of the blunt before security came. You know, get nice."

"I am getting nice. I do me and you do you."

Ana shoved the remaining cocaine Apple's way.

"Come on, we don't have all night."

Apple quickly took the coke and laced her blunt. The minute she lit up, the putrid smell permeated the whole bathroom. Apple took a couple pulls—which was all she really needed—and put the blunt out and slipped it back into the EZ Roll package.

Moments later, the girls came out the stall, high and glassy eyed. They received a few sideway looks from the other girls.

Apple scowled back and barked, "Y'all bitches got a fuckin' problem?"

They didn't respond. They didn't want any trouble. They left the bathroom shaking their heads.

Apple and Ana went to the mirror and touched up their makeup. While putting on her lip gloss, Ana, out of the blue, asked, "You gonna fuck Tony tonight?"

"What! No! He's just a nigga I'm having some fun with. If he's stupid enough to give us free drinks and coke, that's his dumb ass."

Ana laughed. "He's cute, though."

"And I got a man. I'm not trying to cheat on your brother. Why don't you fuck him?"

"I'm like you," Ana said. "Just taking advantage of a good time."

As if on cue, Apple's phone rang. It was Jamel calling. "Speak of the devil," she said to Ana.

She answered while Ana still primped in the mirror and combed her hair.

"Hey, baby," Apple said, smiling heavily.

"Where you at?"

"I'm at the club with your sister. Why?"

"I wanna see you tonight," he said.

"You wanna see me tonight? Aaaah, you miss me, baby?"

"I do," Jamel said.

Apple smiled. She definitely wanted to spend some quality time with her man. Hearing his voice always excited her. Even after the bullshit he put her through, she was still in love with him.

"Where you at?" she asked.

"I'm at the apartment in Brooklyn. Don't have me waiting long."

"Okay, I'll be there, soon," Apple said. Jamel had perfect timing. Horny from the blunt and alcohol, she was ready to run to him.

"I see you about to get you some," Ana said dryly.

Apple smiled. "And the partying continues."

The girls walked out of the bathroom and into the thick crowd again. As they moved toward the exit, forgetting about Tony and his friends,

Apple suddenly felt someone grab at the back of her arm, trying to prevent her from walking away. Annoyed, she and Ana turned around.

"Where y'all going?" Tony said. "I know y'all ain't about to leave."

"Yeah, we're leaving," Apple said.

"What! Y'all trying to leave now when shit is just getting started? I thought we were having fun."

"It was fun while it lasted, but I got a man to go home to," Apple said, staring at Tony unflinchingly.

Tony twisted up his face. "Your man! Bitch, you ain't talk about your man when you were drinking champagne in VIP and sniffing free blow."

"Thank you, but that was your dumb ass wanting to trick on us. And I don't sniff blow, bitch!"

"You was supposed to leave with me tonight. Come on, ma. You know how shit go down up in the club."

"What? You thought we were going to fuck tonight? Nigga, please!"

Tony glared at Apple. His crew stood behind him, looking like they were ready to react physically. Bitches or no bitches, they were riled up from the liquor in their system and were ready to thrust themselves into any altercation.

Suddenly, there was a tense standoff inside the club.

Apple and Ana glared at Tony, knowing he was upset and disrespected.

Tony yelled, "Fuck you, bitch! You owe me."

"Nigga, I don't owe you shit! And believe me, I'm not the bitch to fuck with. My man will come down here and murder all y'all niggas."

"What, bitch? You know who the fuck you talking to?" He reached out and grabbed Apple's arm roughly.

She quickly yanked herself back, jerking free from his grip. Then she spat in his face and shouted, "Nigga, don't put your fuckin' hands on me!"

Tony couldn't control himself. He lunged at her with force. He wanted to break her face in half.

Apple struggled against him. She kicked out her right leg trying to smash her heel against his balls, but her movements were far too slow.

Tony's people went after her too, but Ana quickly stepped into the melee and started swinging wildly like she was Laila Ali in the ring.

"Get the fuck off my bitch!" Ana screamed out. She was a female, but she was feisty and raw.

Tony seized Apple's arms, trapping them at her side. He pushed her roughly against the wall, causing her to stumble and almost fall flat on her face.

Ana tried to take on two at a time, crashing her clutch against their faces, but they overpowered her and knocked her down to the ground. She tried to avoid being trampled by the crowd.

"Get the fuck off me!" she shouted.

Apple went toe to toe with Tony. She balled her hand into a fist and thrust forward.

A sudden rush of pain jolted Tony's body. He was shocked at the wallop Apple packed. He hit back and bloodied her lip.

Soon, security swooped into the melee and physically removed the men off the girls. Security threw in a few punches themselves.

"Those are females!" one bouncer shouted.

Then another fight broke out between the bouncers and Tony's men.

Suddenly the music stopped, and the club lights came on. Clubgoers were looking on at the brawl.

Apple and Ana weren't done yet. They quickly collected themselves and charged behind the bouncers trying to toss out Tony and his crew.

Apple grabbed a beer bottle and broke it against the bar, and Ana did the same. The melee spilled outside into the street. Apple went charging at Tony with the broken bottle clutched in her hand, screaming heatedly, "I'm gonna kill you, muthafucka!"

She was quickly restrained by a nearby bouncer.

Then the inevitable happened. Gunshots rang out, and the crowd quickly scattered like roaches.

Apple noticed a bouncer drop to the pavement.

"What, muthafucka? What?" she heard someone scream out.

"Let's go, Apple!" Ana screamed.

The girls took off running in the opposite direction, their high heels pounding into the pavement. They hopped into a passing taxicab.

"We're making two stops," Apple said out of breath, relieved to get away from all that craziness. "Williamsburg and then Staten Island."

"Yo, that shit was crazy," Ana said, almost looking thrilled how it all played out.

Apple laughed. "I know, right? Fuckin' bitch-ass niggas. He actually thought he was about to get some pussy tonight."

"Stupid muthafuckas! They lucky I didn't have my gun on me."

"I feel the same way. Fuck them niggas! Trying to ruin my night with my man."

Ana chuckled. "Look at you, still trying to get some dick."

"Oh, the show don't stop because some drama popped off, sweetie."

Ana giggled. "I see." She then looked at Apple quietly and then added, "But I got your back, Apple."

"Thanks for that, Ana. I appreciate that."

"No problem. I can tell you're a real bitch like me, and I'm gonna have your back, Apple. You've been cool with me. I respect that."

Apple nodded, taking in Ana's words. The two looked at each other, locking eyes as the cab moved through the city, heading toward the Williamsburg Bridge. A new bond was forged, and Apple felt she had a friend in Ana.

TWENTY

L et me see that one right there," Kamel said, pointing at the diamond bracelet in 18k white gold.

"Beautiful choice," the saleswoman said. She unlocked the case and removed the diamond bracelet.

Kamel took it into his hand and inspected it. It was a lot prettier in his hand. The price tag was $4,200. Pocket change to him.

The saleswoman went on to explain the bracelet in detail.

"The bracelet features brilliant round diamonds set in eighteen karat white gold with a hidden safety catch clasp."

"Nice," Maleek uttered.

"It is, right?" Kamel said.

The saleswoman knew her jewelry. She worked for a local and family-owned jeweler, with stores in three of the five boroughs.

Kamel looked at the bracelet and then turned to Maleek and said, "What you think?"

"I think she's going to love it, Kamel."

"I hope so. She's very special to me, and she deserves the best."

"She's a very lucky woman," the saleswoman chimed.

"No, I'm a very lucky man."

She smiled, transfixed by Kamel's swag and sex appeal. The look in her eyes spoke clearly. If given the chance, she would throw herself at him and do whatever to please him. Kamel considered himself a one-woman man. His player days were behind him; his main concerns were his family and their future.

"I'll take it," he told the lady.

"Great. How will you be paying, cash or charge?"

"Cash." He went into his pocket and pulled out a wad of hundred-dollar bills.

She tried not to stare, but she couldn't help but to look at a wad like that.

Kamel peeled off hundred after hundred and placed it on the table. "That's five grand, keep the change."

She beamed. "Thank you."

"No problem."

She placed the bracelet into a stylish velvet box and had it wrapped for him.

"When you gonna give it to her?" Maleek asked.

"I'm gonna do it this weekend, take her out to a nice restaurant, get a hotel suite and make her feel very special." Kamel was excited and couldn't wait to see the reaction on Kola's face.

Maleek nodded and smiled. He was happy for his friend. He was happy for Kola. He wanted to see the two of them get married. He had seen Kamel go through a lot in the streets. It was about time his friend grabbed a slice of happiness.

The saleswoman handed Kamel the jewelry bag. He thanked her and left. Maleek was right behind him, armed and dangerous.

They walked out of the store and crossed the busy street toward the parked Denali. Maleek got behind the wheel, and Kamel climbed into the passenger seat.

"Where to now?" Maleek asked.

"Take me home. I miss my baby."

Maleek nodded. As he was about to pull off, a black Benz came to an abrupt stop in front of them, blocking their way out. Maleek slammed on his brakes and instantly pulled out his gun.

Kamel snatched the .45 from the glove compartment and cocked it back. "What the fuck!"

All four doors to the Benz opened up, and several men stepped out.

Kamel's eyes started to dance around at everyone. He was trying to stay sharp. Instantly, he knew who they were—the KB Bloods, PJ's gang. They didn't come charging and blazing with guns, which was a good thing, but they did come in force. He knew they were armed and dangerous. Kamel knew it was inevitable that he would run into them. PJ was an important man—a supplier and a respected OG.

They surrounded the truck. Marko, the leader walked toward Kamel's window, the butt of a 9 mm peeking from underneath his jacket. He was tall and slim, clad in a red velour sweatsuit. His cornrows reached shoulder-length, and his eyes were black and bitter. He tapped on the window.

With one hand on the handle of his Glock and the other on the power button to roll down the window, Kamel carefully let the window down. "What's up, Marko?"

"You tell me, nigga. Where's your brother and that bitch?" Marko asked sternly.

"I don't know what you talking about," Kamel coolly replied.

"Kamel, we gonna play these games? I know it was your brother that murdered PJ, and he took that bitch Ana with him. Just give them up and we square, blood."

"First off, I ain't your blood." Kamel hardened his eyes on Marko and then continued, "And, I heard about PJ. My condolences."

"Fuck your condolences, nigga! We want your fuckin' brother," Marko exclaimed loud and clear.

Maleek sat still and calm. He was ready to react, his hand on a Glock also. If it came to it, he would slam his foot down on the accelerator and start shooting and hitting niggas at the same time.

Kamel glared at Marko as he spoke.

"I don't know where my brother is. We don't talk, and I doubt he had anything to do with PJ," Kamel said calmly. "And if I did know, I wouldn't tell. So now what, nigga!"

"Yo, blood, check this, if you don't give up your brother or Ana in a week, I'm comin' after everyone and everything you love. This ain't a game, nigga. PJ was family. Your brother is a foul muthafucka, and you know it, nigga!"

Kamel locked eyes with Marko again. Kamel didn't like the threat thrown his way. His dark, fiery eyes pierced Marko's skin with extreme anger and tore apart his soul—if only looks could kill. Kamel's index finger was on the trigger of the Glock, and it only took a quick second to make a bad situation worse. His eyes narrowed at the man in front of him.

"Like I said, I haven't seen or spoken to him in a while," Kamel said with a harsh tone. "And you think it's smart to threaten my fuckin' family?"

"It ain't smart to murder a friend. But, a'ight, you playin' it like that, Kamel?"

"Yeah, I'm playing it like that."

Both men noticed an NYPD cruiser turning the corner onto the block out of the blue, two officers in the front seat.

Marko didn't want the heat. He backed away from Kamel's truck and said, "I'll see you and your brother around, nigga."

"Yeah. See me, nigga," Kamel retorted.

Marko and his men climbed back into the Benz and drove away, leaving Kamel with a bad taste in his mouth. He blew air out of his mouth and placed the Glock back into the glove compartment and watched the police drive by him.

TWENTY-ONE

Apple was dripping with excitement when she felt the head of Jamel's dick invade her pussy walls. She grabbed the sheet. Jamel was pounding his erection fiercely inside of her. He was being creative, stroking it at every angle, hitting all her spots. Deep in the missionary position, he buried himself inside her and started using his muscles to flex his dick, causing her to lose control.

She was chanting and moaning, "Ooooh! Fuck me! Fuck me!"

Her words were rants of a very horny woman. She had a lot on her mind and needed the release. The fight at the nightclub the other night had turned her on. For three days straight, she and Jamel had been on a sex and drug binge, fucking their brains out and getting blunted.

Jamel sucked on her nipple and cupped her ass. He put her legs vertically into the air and fucked her raw. Then Apple positioned herself on top and started sliding down his hard dick. She knew exactly how to get her pleasure and wasn't afraid to go for it. Jamel was deep inside her and making her spew profanity.

"Ooh! That dick feels so good!" Apple milked his dick, gyrating her hips into him and making her pussy contract.

"I'm gonna cum!" Jamel bellowed.

"Yes, baby, come for me. Ooooh shit, I feel that muthafuckin' dick about to come! Come, baby," she hummed like a musical note.

A few more upward thrusts into her tight, wet pussy, and he exploded like a geyser. They trembled uncontrollably against each other, as Apple felt every bit of his semen discharging inside of her.

After his nut, she rolled off the dick and sparked up a coke-laced blunt.

Jamel breathed out, feeling extremely satisfied, and followed Apple's lead. He did a line of cocaine from the mound of white sitting on the nightstand. "Damn! This some good shit," he said.

"I'm feeling nice."

Apple lay naked, feeling happy and elevated from good dick and good blunts.

Jamel stood up naked, his dick swinging. He lit a cigarette, took a few drags and looked at Apple lying naked on the bed. He asked, "What's up wit' you and Mack D? You still ain't tryin' to see that nigga?"

"I told you, I'm not fuckin' with him," she replied.

"But your sister's gettin' in close, from what you telling me, right? They building some special bond and shit," he said.

"She's looking for something that will never be there."

"What? The bitch got daddy issues?"

"She's making a mistake."

"She's doin' what we need to be fuckin' doing—getting in close and feeling that nigga out. That's a damn move we should be making. He invited you to dinner, and you turned him down. I'm telling you. We can get that nigga, catch him slipping."

"He's not that stupid, Jamel."

"Fuck that! Any nigga could slip up and get got. We just gotta plan correctly, that's all."

Apple still wasn't going for it. She wanted little to do as possible with her ex step-daddy. She didn't trust anything he had to say, and she didn't understand how Kola could fall for it.

Jamel started to pace back and forth like a caged tiger, feeling once his cage was opened, he'd be ready to pounce and attack.

"I'm hungry, baby. I want the crown. I want what that nigga got—his connect, his money, and his peoples. I don't know what kind of game he's playing, but it's 'bout to backfire on his ass. Real talk, baby, we gon' do this!"

"We can do us without fuckin' with him, baby. I learned my lesson long ago with these long, mind-bending plot twists. That's how niggas get killed. When I was younger I was down with toying with people like mice trapped in a maze before I pounced. And each time it backfired. Now I know better. You got an enemy, kill him."

"That's what I'm tryna tell you!" Jamel scratched his ass. "We are gonna dead that nigga, but not right now. We can infiltrate his whole organization and do shit the right way."

"Your way's the wrong way. Please believe me when I tell you that you, me, Kola, and Kamel can murder Mack D now and still live out our lives."

"You don't listen, Apple," Jamel screamed. "You always want to do things without thinking first! You're hardheaded."

"Look who's talking."

"What's that supposed to mean?"

"Look, Jamel. I'm not my sister."

Jamel looked at her and said, "You damn sure ain't."

"What the fuck you mean by that?"

"Nothing. I ain't mean nothing by it. I just want us to come up."

"We already up, baby," Apple said. She removed herself from the bed and went to placate her man with her nakedness and sexuality. She wrapped her arms around his waist, her breasts pressed against his back. She nestled her head against his roughness, then reached downward to stroke his flaccid manhood.

Jamel seemed unfazed by her soft touch and soothing approach. He stared out the bedroom window and said, "I lost a lot when I lost Mack D as my connect. It's drying up for me out there, so I gotta do what I gotta do to make my ends. You feel me?"

"I feel you, baby."

"Apple, this real talk. To get that paper we had to knock off a few of Mack D goons. That's how I'm eatin' right now."

"So you been robbing Mack D?"

"Don't act like you above that shit. Not that long ago you was ski-masked up in B-more for that paper."

"You just as dumb as Kola! Why don't anybody want that nigga dead except me!"

"Be easy, ma. If I kill the cash cow that means no more milk money for you."

"You think this is a game?"

"I do. A game I plan on winning with my sexy bitch by my side."

Apple began to soften. "Promise you won't let this get out of hand."

Jamel nodded. "You got my word."

Apple embraced Jamel from behind and kissed the back of his neck. Despite all the drama he put her through, she would have laid down her life for him, and she hoped he'd do the same. Their passion bonded them together, and their knack for violence and street savvy solidified that bond.

She whispered into his ear. "I want you again."

She guided him back to the bed before straddling him and guiding his erection to her opening. She slowly descended against him, moaning from his raw penetration. She started to slowly move herself against him, winding and gyrating her pelvis into his lap, her tits in his face. She closed her eyes and grabbed his shoulders and fucked him like a porn star, riding his cock with whatever pace she wanted.

Jamel grabbed her ass and worked her body into his. He then arched himself away from her, his arms extended behind him, his hands flat against the bed, and allowed Apple to do all the work.

The two finished off with multiple orgasms and ejaculations with Jamel doing more and more blow.

Bam! Bam! Bam!

Hard knocks at the door quickly got Jamel's and Apple's attention. They both perked up and were immediately on high alert.

"Who the fuck is this?"

Jamel jumped out of bed and grabbed his 9 mm Beretta. He cocked it back and didn't bother to get dressed as he walked to the door naked. Apple was right behind him.

The heavy knocking continued.

Jamel looked through the peephole and sighed with relief. He opened the door in his birthday suit, and barked, "Nigga, what the fuck you doin', knockin' on my fuckin' door like you the fuckin' police?"

Mark-Mark walked inside. "We got a problem?"

"What kind of problem?" Jamel asked.

Mark-Mark wasn't bothered by Jamel's nakedness. He had seen worse. He kept a straight face and said, "Zink is dead. They found his body in the park, his fingers missing and shit. They sayin' it's a message."

"And what that got to do wit' me? That's your boy."

"Word on the streets is that Mack D got two corrupt detectives on his payroll and he got them hunting down the niggas that stole from him."

Jamel wasn't offended by Mark-Mark using the word *nigga*. It was business with them, and Mark-Mark was a cool white boy he could trust.

"You think I'm scared of that faggot? His own peoples stole from him, and we stole from them? A quarter of a million is a good come-up," Jamel said. "You scared, nigga?"

"Nah, I ain't scared, just cautious. I don't underestimate anyone. I'm always on guard twenty-four/seven," Mark-Mark said.

"And you should always be. It's a jungle out there, and we gonna be the predators eating off the prey," Jamel stated with a wry smile.

Mark-Mark nodded. He then noticed Apple standing in the hallway listening to their conversation in Jamel's T-shirt, her shapely legs on display.

"She cool, right?" Mark-Mark asked.

"Yeah, she's cool."

"A'ight."

"But you know you interrupted something important for some bullshit. I ain't worried about Mack D or any corrupt cops. We got our money, and we got away clean with it. If niggas is stupid enough to steal for us, then they deserve to get got. But holla at me later, nigga. We'll talk." Jamel gave Mark-Mark dap and let him be on his way.

When the door closed, Apple walked toward him and asked, "Is everything okay?"

"Yeah, everything's cool. But you know what would be even better?"

"What's that?"

"If you crawl back in bed and spread your legs open wide and let me eat your pussy out."

Apple grinned. And then did as she was told.

TWENTY-TWO

Kola had breakfast ready for the kids—grits and eggs along with biscuits and fruit. The kitchen smelled like a soul food restaurant, and Kola looked like Susie homemaker in a blue apron and oven mitts. The kids came running in with their morning appetites and took their places at the table.

"It smells so good," Peaches said.

"And everything is going to taste good too," Kola said, smiling. She opened the oven door and removed a plate of fluffy biscuits that made the kids' mouths water from just the sight of them.

Peaches and the siblings immediately dug into their food, fattening their faces. For a moment, Kola stood by and admired her handiwork. Seeing the kids stuff their faces with her cooking made her feel so motherly.

"It tastes good," Sophia said.

"I'm glad you like it, Sophia."

Kola had so much planned for them. The kids weren't in school yet, but she was working on that. Kamel had a friend who could falsify birth certificates, social security numbers, and transcripts. The plan was to temporarily get the children into school to keep them active and educated. Since the siblings were illegal in the country, it was a challenge to transition them into US citizens, but she was working hard at it. Their English was better, and they were adjusting better than she thought they would.

The house was becoming a home, and it was one big happy family. Peaches was talkative, laughing and interacting with her surrogate brother and sister.

"And today I want you and Eduardo Jr. to draw some pictures for me to send to your mommies and daddy, okay?"

"Okay," both Eduardo Jr. and Sophia replied.

Suddenly, trouble walked in the kitchen clad in a small white T-shirt that barely covered everything. Ana looked like she was having a hangover.

Kola frowned and looked at her like she was an animal trying to snatch away one of her cubs.

"Damn!" Ana said. "What you cooking smells good and shit."

"We don't have enough," Kola belted out sharply. "And put some clothes on."

Ana sucked her teeth and frowned. "What? Because of that little nigga? He gotta start seeing some pussy at some point of his life. Why not now?"

Kola suddenly charged Ana's way and slapped her so hard, she almost spun her into next week. She hit the floor, stunned by the attack.

"You watch your mouth around them!" Kola exclaimed heatedly.

Peaches and the others were shocked by what they saw.

Kola didn't mean to attack Ana in front of the kids. She reacted without even thinking about it.

Ana jumped up from the floor and went after Kola with her fists, swinging wildly, but missing her mark by a mile.

Ana was a fighter, but she couldn't compete with Kola. It took only two hits to knock her back down to the kitchen floor.

"Don't do this in front of them," she pleaded to Ana.

"Fuck you!" Ana screamed out.

Sophia started to cry, Peaches looked on in shock, and Eduardo Jr. was quiet and looking scared.

With perfect timing, Apple walked into the house after having a great time with Jamel. She quickly stepped in between Ana and her sister. "What the fuck! What's going on with y'all?"

"That bitch attacked me!" Ana shouted.

"She needs to watch how she dresses and talks in front of the kids, especially Peaches, your *daughter*," Kola said, emphasizing *daughter*, so Apple could get the hint.

Apple didn't know what to think. It was clear that her sister had gotten the better of Ana.

Kola grabbed Peaches and the kids and told them to go to their room.

"Kola, you be tripping for no reason." Ana rubbed the side of her face. "What did I do to deserve you coming for me like that?"

Ana was good at playing the victim. She could turn it on or off quickly.

Kola looked at Ana and said, "You need to watch your mouth around those kids." She sighed. "But I'm sorry for putting my hands on you. It won't happen again."

Ana was still tight-faced. She didn't accept the apology. She wanted to ram her fist into the back of Kola's head.

Kola looked at Apple. Her pupils were wide and dilated, even in a well-lit room. Her eyes were bloodshot-red.

Kola shook her head in disgust at her sister. "You're high, aren't you?"

She thought high meant Apple smoking too many blunts and tossing back too many shots of Henny. Kola had no idea the blunts were laced with cocaine. She would have been even more furious.

"I don't have time to deal with y'all two. I gotta get the kids ready and take them shopping today. Someone has to be a parent around here and think about them." She stormed out of the kitchen leaving Apple and Ana to themselves.

Ana looked at Apple and said, "You see that?"

"See what?"

"How she talks to you, like she's better than you or something."

Apple didn't seem upset about it, but Ana continued talking.

"You're Peaches' mother, but from the looks of things, I couldn't tell. And y'all twin sisters, the exact same age, and she belittles you like you're a child. What? She thinks that she's better than you because you like to get high and have fun? Apple, you know her better than me, and I know Kola did her dirt too. So what gives her the right to look at you sideways and judge you?"

Ana's words left Apple pondering a few things. Kola wasn't better than her, but growing up, Kola always felt that way. Most times, Kola thought that her shit didn't stink. Even now, she wanted to take charge over everything. From the household to the streets, she was trying to be some kind of superwoman and receive all the credit.

That was Kola, always trying to fix something and stamp her name on it. She'd met with Mack D when Apple was against it, and was tending to her daughter without her involvement. Apple knew she could be a better mother to Peaches than her sister any day.

"I'm just sayin', you're a good chick, and your sister needs to know that," Ana added. "Don't let her turn your own daughter against you."

"She would never do that."

"Really? Aren't you the one who told me she had your daughter calling her mommy?"

"That was different. She thought I was dead."

"So what? Even if you were dead what gives her the right to completely erase your memory from your daughter? That's some calculated, fucked-up shit if you ask me."

"Enough!"

Ana smiled. This was too easy.

Things in the house were turning sour. Slowly but surely, the twins were becoming rivals again. Apple's drug use, along with Ana's and Jamel's, didn't help their situation. Apple and Kola started to argue more and more, especially around the kids. Ana was constantly in her ear, being manipulative. Then she'd just simply sit back and enjoy the show.

Apple had something to say about everything Kola did for Peaches.

Kola made breakfast for the kids. Apple made it an issue.

Kola bathed Peaches. Apple made it an issue.

She took the kids shopping or out to the movies. Apple made it an issue. When Kola spent time with her niece and the children, Apple griped.

"I can take care of my own child. You always rushing to try and beat me at every fuckin' thing. You're keeping me from being a mother to my own daughter," Apple barked.

Kola screamed, "If you was taking care of your child rather than running the streets, partying, getting high, and fucking that loser, then you wouldn't have to worry about me parenting your daughter. But I love her, and she needs both of us."

"Fuck you, Kola! You always thought you was better than everyone, even when we were kids growing up, like you're the goose that lay golden eggs. We both came out of Denise's pussy at the same time, so what makes you superior to me?"

"You are impossible, Apple, so fuckin' impossible. Do you know that? Right now your daughter doesn't need her mother and aunt arguing. She needs love and to be cared for. You don't think that poor child has been through enough? Huh? You think this, what we're doing here, will make it any better? These kids' lives are in danger because of the dumb shit your man did! My life is in danger because of the dumb shit your man did! And instead of you giving a fuck, you in here throwing up the past. You and that bitch are so stupid and ignorant! And I'll be damned if I let you take away the happiness that we have left."

Kola pivoted and walked away.

Apple shouted, "I know how to be a mother to my daughter! You hear me, bitch?"

Kola ignored her and went into the bedroom to get away from the drama. She knew the root of the trouble. Ana and Jamel were like two cancers eating away all that was good. She wanted to get rid of the two of them.

But how could she when they were both family to Kamel?

TWENTY-THREE

The view of Central Park from fifteen stories high was breathtaking. The deluxe hotel suite Kamel had reserved for them at $3875 a night was even more beautiful. It had a particularly large private terrace that allowed for unfettered views of the park and the sprawling city. The interior design featured traditional Moroccan lanterns and mosaic tile work throughout. The Jacuzzi was deep, and the amenities seemed endless. The place felt like they had stepped into a completely different country far away from their own.

"Ohmygod, this is so beautiful," Kola said.

"I'm glad you love it," Kamel said with a happy smile. "Tonight, I want it to be just you and me. No interruptions."

She smiled too, and they kissed.

The kids were with a neighbor Kola had befriended after she'd moved into the house. Ms. Kendricks was an affable grandmother of six. She and Kamel trusted her to watch the children overnight. Kola didn't trust Apple with her own daughter, and she definitely didn't trust Ana.

"Beautiful, I'm gonna make a quick phone call, and then after that, it's just you and me, alone and enjoying each other. I have a surprise for you."

"I'm in no rush, baby. Oh, I so needed this. I'm gonna go take in this view of the city and then go change into something sexy for you," she said. "I hope you're ready for me."

"Oh, baby, I'm ready. Believe me."

Kamel went into another room to make his call while Kola stepped out onto the balcony. She enjoyed the breeze and the sun. Below, the city flowed in its tense way, bustling and honking. So many floors up, she was a passive observer, not troubled by its strife.

As she lingered on the balcony and took a deep breath, her cell phone vibrated. She looked at the caller ID. It was Mack D calling. She immediately sent it to voice mail.

"Not today," she told herself. Today was only about her and Kamel. She didn't want to deal with him, Jamel, Ana, and definitely not Apple.

She stepped into the suite and went into the bathroom to change for her man. She couldn't wait to get intimate with Kamel. Just the two of them, building castles in the sky, making love through the night.

Kola stepped out of the bathroom sexily clad in a hot pink Unwrap Me Satin Bow Teddy with a strappy thong back. She stood sexy in a pair of six-inch stilettos and all dolled up from head to toe.

"You ready to unwrap me and get your gift?" Kola said with a teasing smile.

Kamel was in complete awe, blown over by his woman's beauty and sexy outfit. "Damn, baby! I'm so ready. Christmas definitely came early this year."

Kamel was shirtless in a pair of boxers. On the nightstand was a bottle of Dom Pérignon and two long-stemmed glasses. Rose petals covered the bed and the floor, and John Legend's "All of Me" played from the small Beats Pill speaker.

"You're beautiful," he said to his goddess.

"Thank you, baby. This is only for you; your eyes only."

"I know, I know," he replied excitedly.

Kamel stood up and approached his stunning woman. Her eyes were like two rare gems, each time more beautiful with every glance. His hand slid around her waist, and he pulled her close to his pine-scented body. He brushed her hair back from her shoulder and moved in so close, she could feel his lean body pressed against hers. He placed kisses on her shoulders and in her hair.

She wanted his lips now. She wanted his kisses. She wanted to taste Kamel's breath and be sucked into his soul.

Kamel cupped Kola's face into his hand and gave her what she wanted. They kissed fervently, pressing their lips tightly together. They could feel each other's warmth.

A hand ran through her hair, as their kisses became harder.

Kamel then pulled himself away from her sexiness and said, "I have something for you." He pulled out the jewelry box and showed her the diamond bracelet.

"Oh my God, it's beautiful! I love it, baby."

Smiling, he then clasped it around her wrist. It was perfect on her. She admired the diamonds and how it sparkled against her skin. She threw her arms around his neck, and they kissed deeper.

Kamel's hands roamed freely over her curves, gently caressing her small waist and sexy bottom. He was so hard, it almost hurt.

They then sipped champagne and caressed each other on the bed.

Kamel freed himself from his boxers before untying the bow on Kola's teddy.

"I want you," she whispered in his ear. .

They wrapped themselves into an intimate position. Kamel sat lotus-style, while Kola sat into his lap facing him, her breasts pressed against his chest. She wrapped her legs around him, and they wrapped their arms around each other for support. He kissed the side of her neck while thrusting himself inside of her.

They soon came together and collapsed on the bed. After catching their breaths, they started having pillow talk.

"Let's just do it—Go and get married and leave here. I don't wanna stay engaged to you forever; I want you to become my wife."

"Where do you wanna go?"

"Away from New York. Maybe the Caribbean, Hawaii—I always wanted to see Hawaii—or even Africa."

She chuckled. "Africa?"

"Yeah. Why not Africa?" he said. "That would be a great place of us and the kids to start over. Who would come look for us in Africa?"

"It sounds great. As long as I got you in my life, I'll move anywhere," Kola said sincerely.

He smiled, she smiled, and then they embraced each other passionately and kissed. The remainder of the night was spent making love, talking and planning, and making more love.

TWENTY-FOUR

There was loud yelling followed by slamming doors in the house. Kola and Apple had gotten into another huge argument and were close to throwing punches at each other. Thankfully, Kamel was there to defuse the conflict. The kids were with Ms. Kendricks and her grandchildren.

Apple didn't like that Kola sent her daughter to a neighbor's house without her permission. Kola felt she didn't need her permission. Yes, Apple was Peaches' mother, but Kola had been raising and taking care of her since she found her. Apple was getting in the way—disturbing her youth and happy home.

Of course, Ana had to put her two cents in, siding with Apple. Kola was sick and tired of her. She was an inch close to beating the bitch down so seriously, she knew she would get an attempted murder charge.

A few days earlier someone had the audacity to put Neat hair remover in Kola's hair conditioner. Thank God, she had smelled the pungent odor before she'd applied it to her scalp. She blamed Apple, but she denied it. The tension in the house became so thick, it was almost unbearable.

Kola had stormed into her bedroom, and Kamel chased behind her. She was fuming, ready to break up the bedroom, put her fist through the mirror, punch a hole through the wall—do something to release her frustration.

"Baby, calm down," Kamel said.

"I don't like that bitch," Kola shouted, referring to Ana. "She needs to go."

"I'll talk to her."

"You better do something, because I'm so close to beating her down."

Kamel stepped closer to her. He tried to calm her down with his soothing tone and calm demeanor. He wrapped his arms around her and kissed the side of his neck. "Don't worry about them, baby. Just worry about us. I'm here and I got your back." He kissed the side of her neck again and held her in his arms, trying to calm his boo down.

She was still seething, but his words and comfort were cooling her anger. His presence against her was so alluring and enticing. He squeezed her and was ready to please her. Their bedroom was like a haven away from everything that was poison to their world.

Kola spun around in his arms and locked eyes with him. The look he had, it was definitely love all around.

"Nobody gonna fuck with you, baby. I will die for you," he said wholeheartedly.

Kola remembered how they'd met in the strip club. It felt like he was stalking her, but for Kamel, it was love at first sight.

She had a preconceived notion about him; thought he was a brute idiot and an asshole like the others. But she was wrong about him, and she was so happy that she gave him a chance.

They kissed passionately. They wanted to tear each other's clothes off and fuck each other's brains out, reenact their lovemaking like at the hotel. But it was a busy day, and Kamel had to meet up with Jamel and handle business. It was business that he didn't want to rush into.

He pulled away from her and smiled. "To be continued."

She laughed. "Oh, it's like that?"

He kissed her. "For now, yeah. I can't spoil you with too much good dick. I want you to want my dick twenty years from now."

Kola laughed. "Baby, I'm gonna love you a hundred years from now."

"I know we gonna be two old, decrepit lovers still getting hot and nasty. Baby, they ain't gonna know what to do with us when we a thousand years old."

"I know, right?"

He kissed her again.

She didn't know how he did it, but he was able to take her mind off the drama and had her smiling and laughing. It's why she fell in love with him. "I love you," she said.

"I love you too."

Kamel left, and Kola went about making the kids some dinner.

An hour later, she had macaroni and cheese cooking, along with meatloaf and string beans. She was becoming skillful in the kitchen, doing whatever it took to keep her man happy and the children fed.

She no longer thought about the things she did back in the days. She didn't care for the street life anymore, and she wanted to forget how she lived in Colombia. Living a modest and unassuming life in Staten Island surprisingly fit her just fine. She was working on trying to maintain her happy life.

It'd been weeks since she'd heard from Eduardo, and her relationship with Mack D was strengthening. She was slowly winning him over. They'd met several more times, and the last two times she wasn't frisked. Good sign.

The house was quiet. The children were still at the neighbor's. Apple had gone off to clear her head, but there was still one poison remaining. While Kola was cooking in the kitchen, Ana walked in. Kola glared at her.

Ana raised her hands in the air and said, "I come in peace."

"What do you want?" Kola growled at her.

"Look, I just came to apologize to you," she said humbly.

"Apologize?"

"I know we got off to a rocky start, and things have been crazy between you and me, but I'm sorry. I just miss home, and I've been grieving over my boyfriend. I have a lot going on, and I took my frustration out on you."

Kola didn't say a word back. She looked at her. She didn't trust her, no matter what kind of nice shit was spewing from her lips.

"I respect you, Kola. I do. You're a real woman, and I see why my brother is in love with you."

Kola remained silent. She looked in Ana's eyes and saw emptiness and something cruel. There were so many things she didn't like about her.

Kola had been noticing the weird attraction Ana had toward Kamel. Whenever Kamel was at the house, Ana wanted to be up under him, and when he was hungry, she would quickly jump to fix him a plate. Kola would cut in quickly, insisting that she was able to cook and make her man his meal. She'd bark at Ana, telling her to have a seat and that she had everything under control.

Kola wanted Ana to go home. She couldn't put her finger on it, but she was very uncomfortable when Ana was around Kamel. It wasn't overt, but it was underlying, which was confusing. Why would a sister be attracted to her own blood? That was sick.

"When are you leaving?" Kola asked her.

"As soon as Kamel tells me I'm safe, I'm gone. I promise."

That could take forever, and Kola didn't have forever.

Ana continued talking. "What you do around here, it's definitely love. I can see it written all over you. Apple, she should definitely be grateful that you're in her life, the way you're taking care of Peaches. There aren't too many women out there like you. And if I had a sister like you, I would appreciate her."

"Look, bitch, I don't fuckin' like you! I know what you're trying to do, and it's not working. You're poison, and you bring nothing but strife and drama into this house. You may be Kamel's little sister, but you ain't family to me, and you never will be. You think I'm stupid? You think I don't know you're trying to drive a wedge between me and my sister? I'm not going to allow it. Do you fuckin' understand me? You just need to pack your shit and get the fuck out my house!"

Ana stood there looking dumbfounded by Kola's remark. It came unexpectedly while she was trying to play nice. Kola had quickly pulled her card and read her like an open book.

"If I'm not mistaken, I thought this was my brother's house," Ana remarked with a smirk.

Kola was ready to slap her eyes into the back of her head.

Kola continued glaring at her. "I'm not my fuckin' sister," she said with finality.

"I see that," Ana replied under her breath.

Ana was fuming that Kola busted her out and knew she was up to no good. She turned and walked out of the kitchen.

TWENTY-FIVE

Kamel thought about the special night he had with Kola. He was going to remember it for the rest of his life. She was definitely the one, and he wanted to immediately implement what they'd talked about at the hotel. Retiring from the game and leaving the United States with the kids was a great idea. They thought about going to the Caribbean, or maybe Africa, the Motherland. Escaping away to either place sounded like the perfect getaway. Kamel had a few hundred thousand dollars set aside, fake passports, and other important credentials he would need if shit hit the fan and he had to go on the run. Every criminal needed a way out—an escape plan. Kamel was smart enough to know that nothing lasted forever; too bad his brother didn't think the same way.

Forces out there were trying to prevent him from living happily ever after with his fiancée and the kids. One new threat was Marko and his thugs. Word on the streets was the KB Bloods were at war with the twins—shoot and kill on sight. This put Kamel's family at risk.

He contacted his brother and told him about his run-in with Marko.

Jamel's reply was, "You already know, bro—he a killer like you and me. Either you make him go away, or he gonna try and make us go away. PJ was loved and respected. They ain't gonna never forget."

Kamel knew his brother was right. So the two hatched a plan to strike first. Jamel was ready to kill Marko on sight, but Kamel wanted the hit to be more calculated and less dramatic. They already had enough to deal with and didn't need any backlash.

Kamel pulled up to his apartment building in Williamsburg. He left the rented Chevy idling. Clad in all black, wearing a pullover hoodie and combat boots, he smoked his cigarette and waited for his brother to show up. The 9 mm he carried was clean; serial numbers scratched off. After the job he planned on disposing of the gun. It'd been a moment since he'd gotten his hands dirty like this, but he didn't trust anyone else to do it.

Jamel exited the building coolly and approached the car. He got in the passenger seat smiling at his brother. He gave him dap and was ready to get the party started. Jamel was a fanatic when it came to shit like this.

"You ready to do this?" Jamel asked.

"Yeah, I'm ready."

"Let's end this nigga," Jamel said excitedly.

Kamel looked at his brother and the feeling that he was responsible for PJ's demise was still there. Every bone in his body knew the truth. Jamel had been lying to him. The past three months had been nothing but bloodshed from his end. He was going insane. Eight homicides in the city were linked back to Jamel, but the cops couldn't charge him with anything, since there was no evidence or witnesses to indict him on.

Before Kamel pulled off to handle their business, he set his eyes on his brother and said, "What the fuck is wrong with you? You know that everything you do has consequences? Your name is ringing out here too much, nigga, and you're pissing a lot of people off."

"Fuck them! They pissing me off!" Jamel retorted.

"What is your end game with this, Jamel?"

"Nigga, I got a plan. Trust me."

Kamel shot back, "Trust you? You gonna get all of us killed."

"With what I got planned, we gonna wear the crowns soon and be the kings of New York."

Kamel didn't care to wear any crown or become the king of anything. The only thing he wanted to do was love his woman, start his own legal business, and live happy someplace far away from New York.

"Fuck the crown and fuck this life!" Kamel said.

"You're changing on me, bro. Is it her? Kola? Fuckin' ya head up with foolishness? I remember when we had dreams to run this city. You remember, you and me being bosses? Untouchable?"

"Yeah, I remember," Kamel replied dryly. "But people and things change."

"Change, huh? Now you wanna switch up on your only family, especially now. I do have an end game, bro." Jamel lit a cigarette and took a few drags. "I got something special lined up. I linked up with these Armenians—"

"Armenians?" Kamel questioned with a raised eyebrow.

"Yeah, Armenians, and I set up a sweet deal with them. We needed a new connect. I found one. Only one problem. They want a million-dollar buy in."

"A million?"

"Yeah, nigga, a fuckin' million. These niggas don't come cheap, and they're ready to supply us with some high-quality shit. The problem, these muthafuckas don't trust or like niggas like that, so they want their money up front. I start a business relationship with them, and we on our way to becoming major suppliers in this fuckin' city. So I'm doin' whatever it takes to get this money up."

The plan sounded asinine to Kamel. No one pays 100% before delivery of product. He didn't want any dealings with them. Jamel was becoming a megalomaniac—he was ready to kill his way to the top. They were going down very different paths.

Kamel didn't want to hear any more about it. He knew there was no changing Jamel's mind. Jamel's arrangement with the Armenians looked like it would fall apart like a building collapsing, and the outcome would probably be dust and smoke, many dead.

He put the Chevy in DRIVE and drove away.

An hour later, they watched Marko socialize with his crew and some ladies on the Brooklyn corner. Everyone was drinking and laughing, enjoying the night. The brothers watched Marko's every movement from half a block away. They were waiting for the right time to strike.

"Did you do it?" Kamel asked his brother out of the blue.

"Do what?"

"Did you kill PJ? Be honest with me."

"For Christ sake, I told you I didn't touch that nigga. How many times you gonna ask me?"

"Don't get all worked up. I was just asking."

"Don't fuckin' ask again, Twin. You starting to piss me off."

Jamel continued smoking. He was itching to kill Marko. He never liked the asshole. Marko always thought he was the big bad wolf, because he ran a violent Blood crew. Jamel was ready to show him who the baddest wolf in the city was.

Silence fell between the brothers inside the car. Cigarette smoke filled the air.

Kamel wanted to be patient, but Jamel couldn't wait. He toyed with the Glock and fixed his eyes on the men lingering on the corner. They all were high and tipsy, losing focus, not staying alert, thinking no one was crazy enough to attack them.

"Look at them, fuckin' idiots," Jamel said. "It's too fuckin' easy right now." He took his gun and dry-fired at all his victims. "*Boom! Boom!* One at a time, and problem solved. No more Marko." He laughed.

"Just Marko."

"So you callin' the shots, huh?"

"I just wanna do it right."

"Yeah, I do too," Jamel said.

Ten minutes went by, the brothers still sat and waited. Fewer men were now on the corner. Marko downed a forty and held court. Four men to deal with.

"Fuck this!" Jamel uttered, suddenly leaping from the vehicle with the Glock in his hand.

"Jamel, what the fuck! Not now!"

His brother refused to listen.

Jamel hurried toward the crowd, ready to execute everyone standing around Marko. Kamel didn't have a choice but to follow behind him. The brothers were in the dark, hoods concealing their identities.

Jamel fired first, his gun exploding into the night.

Kamel outstretched his hand and fired away too.

Marko went down first from a bullet slamming into his chest.

Panic quickly ensued. Marko's men tried to scatter, but all three were gunned down by the twins. When the smoke cleared, four lay dead.

They retreated back to the Chevy.

Kamel went berserk. "Nigga, I told you to fuckin' wait! You put my life at risk with your fuckin' ignorance."

"Nigga, fuck waiting! I saw a chance, and I went after it. That's what I do—problem solved!"

Each day, Kamel felt his brother was becoming more insane and harder to manage.

TWENTY-SIX

"Tell me about her—my daughter, Nichols," Mack D said.

"Where do I start?" Kola replied.

"From the beginning."

The two of them were leisurely walking around a suburban park in Long Island, taking in a beautiful fall late afternoon. The places for them to secretly meet were limited. A slight breeze rustled the leaves, making them fall to the ground one by one. The air was unseasonably warm. The pathway they walked on was nothing but dirt littered with random rocks.

Richard and another of Mack D's henchmen were standing patiently by the SUV in the parking lot while their boss had another rendezvous with Kola.

"I miss her so much," Kola said. She sighed and added, "Nichols was such a beautiful girl with an even more beautiful personality. She could walk into a room and light it up with her smile. She was smart. I mean, that Harvard smart, straight *As* and studious. If she was alive today, your daughter, she . . ."

Kola started looking forlorn. Thinking and talking about her baby sister was always hard. The corner of her eyes started to water. Kola looked off into the distance. For a moment her mind took her to a place that she wanted to forget—Nichols' murder.

". . . she would have been somebody. I mean, she would have been educated and lived a good life. I could tell whenever I looked into her eyes that she was going to be different from us."

Mack D was listening carefully. Hearing Kola speak highly about his daughter gave him a warm feeling. He felt Kola's praise was a reflection on him. Mack D wanted to pat his own back for fathering such a smart girl. One of his many regrets was not protecting her from her murderers.

They continued circling the park during their lengthy talk.

"You know, I always tell myself to do something today that your future self is going to thank you for," he said to Kola.

"Well, you did a lot to be thankful for, for the next hundred years or so."

Mack D laughed. "Now I'm going for the next five hundred years."

"If you don't mind me asking, what is your net worth?"

Mack D raised his eyebrow. "You know, that's a bold question to ask."

"I've always been a bold woman."

"Like your mother," he said. "But, roughly, I say my net worth is about a hundred million."

Kola whistled at his statement. "Now that's a lot of bread baking."

"What can I say? I love the dough."

They shared a gentle laugh. They stopped at a pond where a few ducks were swimming around.

Mack D stepped closer to the water. He crouched toward it and dipped his fingers into the pond.

"You know this is one of my favorite places to come and think," he said.

Kola looked around. "Yeah, it's nice here. Quiet."

"Life . . . what can I say about it? You may not always end up where you thought you were going, but you will always end up where you are meant to be."

Kola nodded.

Mack D stood up and looked at her. "Where do you think you're meant to be, Kola?"

"Married and happy."

"You love him, do you? Kamel?"

"I do."

He smiled. "I can see it in your eyes."

"We're gonna start planning our wedding soon," she said.

"A wedding? Oh, wow! I hope I'm invited."

"You are. But he's the one. There's no doubt about it."

"Yes, he is the one, I see."

They walked away from the pond and continued talking. The more time Kola spent with Mack D, the more comfortable she became around him. Mack D was becoming the dad she never had, and a confidant. In fact, she was even thinking about asking him to walk her down the aisle. She didn't know how Kamel would feel about that at all. Mack D was still her secret.

"How is your sister?" he asked.

A frustrating sigh came from Kola. She didn't want to talk about Apple.

"That bad, huh?"

"We were starting to build again and trust each other, then one fool comes into our home with her bullshit and the ripples start to happen."

"I assume it's a problem that you can handle on your own."

"It is."

"Okay."

They started to walk back toward the parking lot, where Richard was waiting. Before they got to the parking lot, just out of the blue, Mack D said, "Have you heard from Eduardo lately?"

Kola was taken aback by the question. She didn't want to hear from Eduardo. Hearing from him most likely meant death for her and her family—a bullet to her head— and she probably wouldn't even see it coming.

"No!" she answered, annoyed that he brought his name up. "Right now, we're at odds with each other. I'm not his favorite person right now, Mack D."

"I assure you, you and your family are under my protection. I'm a very powerful person, Kola. Remember that."

"I haven't forgotten."

"Cool."

Kola still had some doubts. She wasn't a fool to completely buy into it. She was playing along, but at the same time, she had become sucked into Mack D's charming personality.

"I do a favor for you, and you do a favor for me?"

"What kind of favor?"

"I will forever be in your gratitude," he said.

Kola was listening. A part of her didn't like where the conversation was going. They had stopped walking. The park was still, and it was getting late. They were now facing each other, locking eyes.

Mack D came out and said, "I need for you to try and make contact with Eduardo."

"What?" She was shocked that he would ask such a thing. "Why?"

"Hear me out. I have a strong business proposition for you, and him."

"I don't want anything to do with what you're proposing."

"For your well-being, I need you to contact him," he said matter-of-factly.

"For my well-being?" Kola swallowed hard. "Are you threatening me?"

"Relax, Kola. You're my daughter, right?"

"Well I hope you feel that way. I know I admire and care about you."

"So contact Eduardo. Do it for Daddy," he said. "And tell him I'm in the position to make him a very, very wealthy man."

"He's already a wealthy man."

"Kola, young Kola, there's no such thing as too much money. Men like us, we always want more—more money, more power, more time."

Kola didn't want to listen, but Mack D insisted she hear everything he had to say.

"With Eduardo as my connect, I'll be able to supply many states and even distribute internationally."

"And what does he get out of the deal?"

"Another organization on his side. He needs as many allies as possible in this game."

"He's in a Colombian prison."

"And you think that will stop a man like him?"

Kola was against it fully. The last thing on her agenda was connecting Eduardo with Mack D. It would never work. Mack D was grimy, and he would probably try his petty bullshit with Eduardo's people and end up six feet under.

Kola just wanted Eduardo to not murder her and Kamel in their sleep, and to allow her to live her life without peering over her shoulders.

"So, what is your answer? Can you connect me with him?"

She couldn't. He always contacted her, and it'd been weeks since they spoke. She couldn't tell Mack D that. Her connection to Eduardo was her only leverage. A straight "No" from her mouth could mean life or death.

"I'll set it up," she said.

Mack D smiled. "That's my girl."

He turned and started to walk again, and Kola followed behind him. As they walked together, the next thing that came out of Mack D's mouth was very upsetting to Kola.

"You know, I can't understand how you could leave a man like Eduardo in jail and fall in love with a bitch-ass nigga like Kamel. From my understanding, you left your man high and dry."

His comment definitely rubbed Kola the wrong way. She held back her harsh retort and said, "You can't help who you fall in love with."

"I guess so."

For the remainder of their meeting, Kola remained distant and just wanted to get home. Now she was doubly in fear for Kamel's life. What if Mack D murdered Kamel to get in the good graces of Eduardo? Kola had so much on her mind. She needed to do something, but at the moment, she was clueless.

Kola lingered in the backyard smoking her third cigarette. It was late, with a full moon above, and the kids were sleeping. As midnight came trailing, everything wasn't forgotten about the day. She couldn't stop thinking about what Mack D had said to her. A seed of nervousness was digging itself inside of her. It made her clench her fist tightly, until her nails dug into the palm of her hand, but she barely noticed. Kola had a lot on her mind, and so many things were trying to weigh her down and sink her.

She took a few pulls from the Newport burning between her lips and looked lost in confusion. Apple was right about Mack D—he couldn't be trusted. All the time she thought she was playing him, getting him to look at her as his daughter so that he would be in her corner no matter what. She wanted Mack D to be the muscle she was used to having in her corner; a pitbull on a chain that she could let go at any time to get at her enemies. Instead, all the dinners, long talks, and reminiscing about Denise and Nichols was all a rouse. She felt so stupid.

"You okay?" Kola heard Apple say.

Kola turned around slightly. Apple was stepping into the night with her. They both still had their differences, but Apple could tell something was bothering her sister. She stood near Kola and said, "Can I bum a smoke off you?"

Kola stared at her briefly. She was still offended about her attitude lately, but she shared her cigarette with her anyway.

"Thanks, sis," Apple said.

Apple took a few pulls and exhaled. "I know we been having our differences lately, but I know something's on your mind. What you thinking about?"

It took a minute for Kola to speak. But she confided to her sister, saying, "I met with Mack D today."

Apple sighed and asked, "Any closer to your Machiavellian plan?"

"Nope."

"Then why do you keep seeing that man?"

"He needs my help."

"Help with what? Eduardo?" Apple figured out.

"He's been playing me all along. He wants me to connect him with Eduardo to help expand his organization," Kola said.

"That muthafucka needs to go. Tonight! Let's just do it."

"And how we supposed to make that happen, Apple? With what army? You think Kamel and Jamel are built to take on a juggernaut like Mack D? It's too soon."

Kola didn't know what to think, but she knew they had to make their move—either fight or flee. Kola continued to confide in her sister, believing that Kamel's life might be in danger. She had Apple's ear completely. Whatever it took to correct their situation, Apple was 100% down, having her sister's back. They both knew that they had to do something. They'd come a long way, and they would continue fighting and proving those who doubted them wrong.

TWENTY-SEVEN

The man's blood was bright red like an apple, and he bled like a gutted pig. He had been badly beaten as well as severely tortured. He could barely see from his swollen eyes, and all his fingers were removed.

"Juice, stay with me now. We're almost done. You hear me?" Mack D puffed on a cigar and blew the smoke in his victim's face.

Juice's breathing was labored as blood trickled from his mouth. He was surrounded by Mack D's henchmen. His fate was inevitable.

"Where's my fuckin' money?" Mack D asked.

"I-I don't know," Juice stammered.

"You don't know? C'mon, muthafucka, you know something. This shit we did to you, it isn't personal, it's only business. We just want answers and to be able to go home like everyone else. So stop making it so difficult for us. Your toes are next. Talk, nigga, or we can make this shit last forever. I want the third man involved, and I want my fuckin' money."

Mack D stared intently at the victim. He was still hanging on, after everything they'd done to him. "You're a tough muthafucka, Juice. I'll give you that."

"We don't have your money," Juice said.

"Why not?"

"Someone stole it from us," he said, then coughed up blood, some of which almost fell on Mack D's shoes.

Mack D quickly stepped back and frowned. "You better not get any of that on me," he warned.

"He ain't talkin', boss," one of his goons uttered.

"He gonna say something valuable. Two hours of this shit, I want a name, address, and my money." Mack D then took his cigar and extinguished it in Juice's swollen, bloody eye. The man howled loud from the agonizing pain.

"Who stole my fuckin' money from you, Juice? I know you fuckin' know who. C'mon, nigga, don't die in vain. Whoever took from y'all, don't you think they need the same treatment that you're getting? Huh? Don't let them get away with it. Make it fair, Juice, and I promise you they will get much worse."

Juice was slipping in and out of consciousness. He was dying for sure. He looked at Mack D and said, "I'm sorry."

"Don't be sorry. Be smart. Just make it up to me by giving me a name and location."

Mack D was anxious. He knew what he needed was on the tip of his victim's lips.

Then suddenly, Juice uttered the name, "Joey."

"Joey, that muthafucka was part of this shit too?"

Juice nodded his head. Joey was a friend of Mack D's dead son. Mack D treated Joey like he was his own son. He and Damien were close. It disturbed him greatly that Joey was behind the plot to steal from him. Now Joey was a dead man.

"Where is he?"

"I-I-I don't know."

It was okay. Mack D had all the information he needed. "You did good, Juice," he said. He gestured toward Richard.

Richard, with the gun in his hand, stepped behind Juice, pressed it to the back of his head, and squeezed.

Mack D pivoted and marched toward the exit. With the sweep of his sword he was handling his business on the streets. With the stroke of his pen he continued to make million-dollar investments. However, what he wanted most was still beyond his reach.

He was becoming impatient with Kola. He'd been calling her repeatedly, but all of his calls were going to her voice mail, unreturned. He felt she was giving him the cold shoulder and brushing him off. He wasn't any closer to getting in contact with Eduardo and establishing a strong cocaine connection with the Colombians, and that angered him greatly.

Mack D ended the call and said to Richard, "This little bitch wants to play games with me, huh? Looks like I'm gonna have to take back the favors I gave her."

Richard managed to smile. He was itching to take out the twins—both sets.

Mack D expected everybody to bow down to him or face the consequences. And he wanted to teach Kola the hard way to never shun or disrespect him. He planned on being clever about it, by attacking when she didn't see it coming. He felt he had been reasonable to her. Now she chose to spit in his face. He was going to slap back.

TWENTY-EIGHT

I t was the twins' 29th birthday. Jamel wanted to celebrate his birthday in style, party hard like a rock star with bitches, booze, and his niggas. His attitude was, you only live once, so do it big or don't do it at all.

Kamel, on the other hand, wasn't interested in having a big bash. He just wanted to keep things simple by spending some quality time with his woman and the kids at home. He wanted to enjoy his birthday in peace.

Jamel went splurging, first buying a custom-made 2006 Honda CBR 600 F4i—liquid-cooled in-line 4-cylinder motorcycle. That night, he hit the club in the city, sat in VIP with his niggas and groupie bitches, popped bottles, smoked weed, and acted a fool on his birthday. He even got a blowjob in the bathroom and came on the girl's face. It was his night, and he was having the time of his life. Ana was there too, turning things up with her big bro and drinking alcohol like it was water.

Apple strolled into the club clad in a very low cute minidress with six-inch heels. She immediately laid eyes on Jamel and Ana dancing together in the VIP section a little too close for her comfort. Ana was touching her man in a somewhat inappropriate way, her short dress riding up her thighs, almost revealing that she didn't have on any panties. Jamel had the widest smile on his face. It was borderline incestuous to Apple's eyes.

Their show suddenly stopped when Apple made her presence known. She cut her eyes at Ana.

Jamel smiled her way and said, "Hey, babe, glad you came." He was obviously a bit tipsy.

"What the fuck was that?" Apple griped.

"Just having a good time with my sister. No need to fuss."

Ana suddenly looked uncomfortable around Apple. She had a stab of guilt showing in her eyes. "He's just tipsy," Ana said.

Apple glared at them both.

Jamel marched her way with a champagne bottle in his hand. He tried to grab Apple inappropriately, but she resisted, backing away from him. She didn't want to be touched by him at all.

"Don't you owe me some birthday pussy?" he said in front of everyone.

She frowned.

Jamel had one hand grabbing his crotch and the other throwing back the champagne bottle. His goons were all laughing at his crazy antics. They all sat slouching and looking intimidating, all of them killers inside the club.

Apple paid them no never mind. Her only concern was Jamel. She had something special planned for him, but it was all going to shit.

"So what's up, babe? We gonna fuck tonight?" Jamel said frankly. "If not, then you fuckin' up my party."

"Fuck you! You the same immature-ass Twin I met in Baltimore. You's a dumb nigga, and dumb niggas don't last long!"

"Oh, so it's like that, huh? You gonna be a bitch on my birthday?"

Out of the blue, Jamel started dousing her with liquor, completely disrespecting her in front of his crew. She smacked him so hard, his eyes almost went spinning backwards.

Ana stood quietly to the side, not interfering with their business. Right in front of her eyes security came bumrushing through the crowd and broke the altercation up.

Fuming, Jamel shouted, "Fuck this party! I don't need this shit!"

Security didn't need to throw him out. He stormed out of the club and climbed onto his new motorcycle. He started the bike, revved the engine, and sped away, doing sixty mph on the city block.

He hit the FDR like a bat flying out of hell and headed north toward Harlem and the bridge. As he now did seventy mph, a car immediately cut him off and slowed, causing him to hit his brakes quickly.

A little too late veering right, he slammed head-first into the back of the vehicle and went flying into the air. He came plummeting to the ground then slid across the road and slammed into the highway divider.

He blacked out as he heard police sirens approaching.

Apple hurried into the emergency room and desperately searched for Jamel. She'd gotten the call an hour earlier and hurried to go see him. Getting into a serious bike accident on the FDR was a hell of a way to finish off his birthday.

Apple rushed to be by his bedside, but Ana was already there, comforting her brother, talking to him. He was in bad shape. His legs were mangled—one broken, his shoulder was dislocated, and he suffered a series of cuts and bruises. He was hurting, but he was alive.

Apple scowled. Lately, she had been noticing the way Jamel looked at Ana. Something just didn't look or feel right. Ana was his sister, so she wondered where her insecurities were coming from.

She was still furious with him, but she still loved him, and she was always going to love him. But she couldn't tolerate Jamel or Ana at the moment.

Instead of going to see how he was doing, Apple turned around and left the hospital. It looked like Jamel already had all the comfort and love he needed at the moment.

TWENTY-NINE

One week in the hospital, and Jamel was healing fine. He was becoming brand-new again. He wanted to hit the streets running and continue what he started, making his million for the Armenians. It was do or die—now or never. It was a deal he desperately needed to happen. The doctors worked miracles on him, and he felt like a well-built machine, despite the cast on his leg. Jamel knew he was lucky to be alive.

Ana was his most frequent visitor while he was in the hospital. Kamel visited his brother once.

The doctor prescribed him some Vicodin painkillers for his leg, and they discharged him. The first thing he wanted to do was make up for lost time—pussy and business.

His relationship with Apple was strained. She was tired and refused to see him.

Ana became his only crutch. Whatever he needed, she was there to support and make his recovery a lot smoother. She owed him and Kamel her life. Marko was dead. It was safe for her to go back home. During the day she spent her time trying to take care of her brother from another mother.

"Whatever you need, Jamel, I got you," she said.

"You got my back, sis. I definitely owe you."

"You can be an asshole sometimes, but I know you love me."

Jamel began popping excessive pills and tossing them back with vodka Ana sneaked in, most times on an empty stomach. His rambling became scary.

"Shit was crazy! Nigga cut me off and shit. Fuckin' bitch-ass nigga! If I find out who did it, I'm gonna put a bullet in his head. That's what I do, I kill people. I got at least sixty, seventy bodies on my jacket. Who got more? Huh? Who? Not that bitch-ass Kamel!"

"Don't talk like that in here, Jamel. What if Kamel heard you?"

"You think I give a fuck about that pussy whipped nigga?"

"In fact I do. You love him, and I know you do."

"You right, Ana. Fuckin' medication got me buggin', fo' real."

She made him drink some water to wet and cool his parched lips. He stared at her and said, "I done some crazy shit. From bitches to niggas, yo, real crazy."

Ana didn't know if it was the medication he was on, or if he was just having a moment because he'd almost lost his life on that motorcycle, but he started to reveal a few things that should have been kept secret.

A week out of the hospital and Jamel started getting high again. He was addicted to the painkillers, adding cocaine to his weed, guzzling liquor, and when that didn't get him high enough, he began snorting almost a gram of cocaine a day.

His dark personality was getting worse. The accident left him feeling vulnerable. He wanted that cast off. Everywhere he went, he was armed to the teeth and extra cautious. He made enemies everywhere, but he refused to be caught slipping and became more dangerous and deadly.

Ana became his right hand suddenly, and the two became closer. He felt she would see things coming before he did, knowing his drug use was hindering his reflexes.

It was a cold day with the holidays approaching. The kids were excited. Kamel wanted to have a merry Christmas with his family. He was the ultimate father figure for the kids and spoiling them rotten with gifts and love. He and Kola wanted to make arrangements for a spring wedding, and then they wanted to escape far off and never come back. She had been ignoring Mack D for over a month. They had been keeping a very low profile, spending time with the kids and surviving one day at a time.

It was late and cold, everyone was tired from having a busy day in the city, from Times Square, a Disney show at Radio City Music Hall, dinner at a nice restaurant, and shopping. The kids were sleeping in the backseat, and Apple was holding her daughter. The car was quiet. Today had been a fabulous day. Everyone got along, and everyone had fun.

Kola and Apple were somewhat on good terms again, though Apple couldn't help but to be a little jealous of her sister's relationship with Kamel. She loved how he treated Kola, and she wanted that kind of relationship for herself.

Arriving at their place in Staten Island was a great feeling. Everyone wanted to hit the sack and sleep. When they pulled into the driveway, they noticed Jamel's Benz was there. They weren't in the mood to deal with his nonsense. Apple didn't want to see him. Kamel also didn't want to deal with his brother.

Apple carried her daughter in her arms, and Kamel carried the siblings. Kola had the keys. They hurried to get inside from the cold. The house was dark and everyone could faintly hear music playing.

The minute they stepped into the living room, they all caught the surprise of their lives.

Ana was straddling Jamel on the couch, riding his dick cowgirl-style. They were fucking their brains out.

Kamel, Apple, and Kola were completely stunned. Apple let out a vicious roar, which woke all three of the kids.

Apple and Kamel put the kids down and Kola hurried them out of the room as Ana was jumping off the dick. Apple had hell and fury showing in her eyes.

"It's not what you think," Ana said.

Apple had no words to say. She released a guttural cry and charged Ana like a linebacker for the New York Giants. Ana went down hard like a sacked quarterback, and Apple started going crazy on the bitch, punching her repeatedly in the face.

Kola returned from the kids' bedroom and quickly aided her sister and joined in on the beat-down. She stomped Ana as Apple had her pinned.

Ana screamed for her life as the blows bore down on every inch of her petite body. She was no match for the twins' fury.

Jamel hurried to pull his jeans up as chaos ensued around him.

Kamel was disgusted and wanted to kill his brother. "Our own fuckin' sister?" he shouted at Jamel. "Our sister!"

It got loud and chaotic inside the house—Ana screamed, the children all screamed, Jamel and Kamel were screaming, and Apple and Kola were cursing Ana the fuck out. They were calling her all types of names; bitch, slut, whore, freak, sicko, psycho—everything! The sisters were going to kill Ana.

Kamel and Jamel had to pull them apart.

Ana was badly beaten, her lip was busted, and her eye was black-and-blue from the assault. She was still naked and hurt. Ana wanted revenge. She glared at Apple and Kola and heatedly shouted, "Y'all bitches wanna fight me when y'all should be fighting y'all fuckin' selves. Jamel fucked Kola!"

It came out fast and poisonous, like a gunshot crackling in the middle of the night. It was breaking news to Kamel and Apple.

Apple cut her eyes at her sister and exclaimed, "What the fuck is she talking about, Kola?"

Kola was dumbfounded. How did Ana know? It had to be Jamel running his big mouth, and it wasn't even her fault.

Ana smirked at Kola and Apple. "Now what, bitches?"

"I can explain what happened," Kola started to say.

"And say what, bitch?" Apple shot back sharply.

Kamel looked at Kola, both anger and sadness settling on his face. He clenched his fists and contorted his face with more anger.

"I thought he was you," Kola quickly tried to explain.

Kamel was so far gone with jealousy and anger, he didn't want to listen to anything she had to say.

"You fuckin' whore!" Apple shouted at her sister.

"I didn't fuck him purposely; I thought he was Kamel!" she repeated.

Apple wasn't trying to hear her excuses.

Kamel wanted to either walk away or react violently. The second thought was more tempting to him.

Since secrets were suddenly being revealed, Apple looked Kola squarely in her eyes and admitted, "Since we being fuckin' honest up in here, you know what? I fucked Eduardo."

Kola glared back at Apple. Hearing she fucked Eduardo was unsettling news. The day went from good to horrible. The yelling in the living room became so loud, no one could completely hear the other.

Kamel wanted to attack Jamel, and Kola wanted to tear Apple apart.

Ana stood on the sidelines and admired her handiwork. Things were going from bad to ugly in seconds.

"You always been a fuckin' thot, Apple!" Kola screamed out. "I didn't fuck Jamel, he fucked me! I was innocent. Can you say the same!"

The bubble burst, and violence erupted. Kola went after her sister, and Kamel took a swing at his brother and almost took his head off.

The melee in the living room was so loud, the neighbors heard it, and their lights came on.

The kids stood in the hallway crying and screaming while witnessing the fight.

Apple and Kola went crashing into the furniture, while the brothers went pound for pound near the kitchen.

Ana even got her few hits in.

Then, unexpectedly, there was loud knocking at the front door that caught everybody by surprise.

"This is the police! Open up now!"

They had no idea who called the police, but they were there. Suddenly panic started to build up inside of Apple and Kola. They couldn't be fingerprinted. They both were wanted felons with new identifies, and a trip to the local police precinct could result in them spending the rest of their lives in prison.

Kamel noticed the worry on their faces. "Quick, y'all go hide in the back room. I'll take care of this," he said.

Apple dragged Ana into the back of the house to hide her from the police.

"You even open your mouth and I'll make sure it's the last words you take," Apple said while holding a .345 to Ana's head.

The kids remained. When everyone was out of sight, Jamel quickly straightened up the room, while Kamel answered the door. The kids were quiet, looking nervous, sitting on the couch.

"How can I help you, officers?" Kamel asked kindly.

"We received a call about a noise complaint and loud arguing coming from this resident. Do you mind if we come inside?" the cop asked.

"Nah, I don't mind at all."

Kamel opened the door wider and stepped to the side. Sweat was running down his cheeks and he tried to control his breathing. The uniformed cops walked inside cautiously. They looked around, taking in everything. The room looked a mess. Their beady eyes were mistrustful of the twin brothers.

Jamel was looking at the police deadpan. He despised law enforcement and was itching to spill police blood. Trying to hold back his contemptuous attitude, he locked eyes with both cops.

"Sorry for the noise, officers," Kamel said politely. "My brother and I were just having an argument."

"Did it get physical?" Both cops hoped they said yes so they could haul them in.

"Nah, not at all. I mean, when we get upset we break things, not each other. That's my brother, and I love him."

It almost hurt Kamel to say that at this very moment.

"Y'all twins, huh?" the taller cop said.

"Yeah, we are," Jamel replied dryly.

They slowly walked around the living room. "Y'all here alone?" the shorter cop asked.

"Just us two and the kids," Kamel lied.

The cops threw a quick smile at the children.

Peaches sat next to the siblings, keeping them cool and calm. She was very mature for her age. She locked her young eyes on the cops and didn't say a word. She was still shaken up at seeing her mother and aunt fighting.

"What were y'all arguing about?" the taller cop asked.

Jamel wanted to say, "None of your fucking business," but he held his tongue and scowled. He didn't know how long he could keep up the polite and quiet act. Both cops were pushing his buttons. "Just a misunderstanding, officers. But me and my brother worked things out."

"Do you mind if we take a look around?"

Kamel hesitated for a moment. He still kept his cool. He had no idea where Apple and Kola were hiding. But he said, "Nah, it's not a problem."

They stepped closer toward the hallway, their eyes scanning every inch of the room. Then a call came in through their shoulder radio. "Unit 5, there's a 459 in progress at Hylan and Main Street."

"Unit 5 here, en route," the officer responded.

He looked at Kamel. "Keep it down; this is a good neighborhood, nice and respectable people. We don't want to come back here again. If we come back, then everyone's going to jail."

"I understand, officer. It won't happen again," Kamel replied.

After the cops left, Apple, Kola, and Ana came out of the closet in the back bedroom, and things were still tense inside the room.

Jamel and Ana left first. Ana quickly dressed, packed the few things she had there, and swore revenge. She'd only had Jamel bring her there to get her belongings. They both climbed into his Benz, and Jamel drove away fast, nursing his wounds. He felt Kamel only had gotten the better of him because of his motorcycle injuries. If he didn't have the cast on his leg he knew he would have wiped the floor with him.

Apple got on the phone and called a cab. She had nothing to say to anyone inside the room. She wanted to leave.

Twenty minutes later a cab was blowing outside. Apple packed a few things while Kola and Kamel watched her without saying a word. Then surprisingly Apple grabbed her daughter and attempted to leave the house.

Kola tried to stop her, and a shoving match ensued. Kola didn't want Apple leaving with her niece. It was too cold outside, and where would she go? It was too dangerous to take Peaches back to their Manhattan apartment. Especially with Kola ignoring Mack D for so long. But Apple was adamant, pushing her sister out the way and determined to leave with or without Kola's consent.

Apple screamed, "She's my fuckin' daughter, Kola. You have no right!"

Peaches was crying. She was confused. She was in a tug of war between both women.

In the end, Apple prevailed and marched out of the house with Peaches and her belongings in her arms. She got inside the cab and didn't look back.

Kola stood in the doorway looking heartbroken. Her tears trickled down her face. She watched the cab drive away, and her heart fell to the pits of her stomach and felt like it was dissolving in acid.

When the cab was out of sight, she turned and went back into the house. Her troubles weren't over yet.

Kamel was standing behind her, glaring at her, not forgetting what was said—she fucked Jamel. How could she stab him in the back like that and fuck his brother? He was so hurt that he wanted to cry. He couldn't even look at her.

Kola stepped toward him, reaching out to grasp his hand, but he refused to touch her.

He looked to Kola for a rational answer. "Why?"

"I thought he was you," she cried out.

He was bewildered. "Did he say he was me!"

Kola went on to tell him everything about that day. She explained to Kamel that when he went away, Jamel came knocking at their door pretending to be him. She thought Kamel had come home early and forgotten his keys.

"He fucked me," she said. "But it was off, different somehow. He was harsher; I should have known it wasn't you." She went on to say how they had the same tattoos, talked the same, and even smelled the same.

Jamel had his brother's traits down pat, even to his touch. Then she went on to tell him that it wasn't until the next day when he showed up from his trip that she knew she had made a serious mistake and Jamel had tricked her into having sex with him.

"I cried when I knew the truth," she said with her eyes filled with tears.

Kamel stood there and listened. He even shed his own tears while hearing her story.

"Baby, I would never cheat on you. I didn't want anyone to find out, you or Apple. I was hurt and felt disgusted. So I kept it a secret. And my relationship with my sister has always been tricky, and I knew if she found out, then it would be hell again with her." Kola sighed, huge tears streaming down her face.

Kamel was still silent, his look cold and distant toward her.

Kola had no idea what he was thinking. "Can you forgive me? I love you. I love you so much."

Kamel said, "There isn't anything I need to forgive. You were the victim, and my brother is a grimy muthafucka. I can believe he would pull some shit like that because he's done it before."

Kamel was hurt, but he couldn't stay mad at Kola. They embraced. She didn't want to let him go. She knew Jamel had told Ana about them. She wanted to kill that Ana bitch.

"Your brother is fuckin' sick," Kola said. "How could he have sex with his own sister?"

Kamel had to tell her the truth. He admitted, "She's really not our sister, Kola."

"What?" It was all too much to take.

"Not biological anyway," he said. "You see, our parents were best friends. Her father and our father were straight up OGs, ran a fierce crew and held the streets down. Her mother was killed when she was eight, and then her father was murdered. She's been in our lives since she was eleven. Her father was like an uncle to me, until someone murdered him. And then someone murdered my father. We grew up together. We were a family."

Kola was listening.

Kamel added, "I had no idea Jamel and her were fucking, I swear."

She believed him.

Kamel always felt that Ana had a strong crush on him, but he refused to cross that line. His brother was a different story. He was a nasty, perverted dog, and Kamel hated they shared the same face and DNA.

All was forgiven between Kola and Kamel, but forgetting would take time. Kamel promised he would always be honest with her, and Kola did the same. Their trials and tribulations were only making their bond stronger.

With Apple, it was a different story. Kola couldn't get the image of Apple fucking Eduardo out of her mind. She wanted to know why and how it happened. She wanted the details. It made her hate Eduardo even more. She wanted him dead. It made her despise her sister again.

The next day, Apple called and left word to them that she was staying at the Marriott in the city, and she planned on coming for the rest of her and Peaches' belongings.

Kola gathered up all of her sister's shit and had a bonfire in the back. *Come get your ashes, bitch!*

THIRTY

I t was the only place left that Jamel could call home—Ana's house in Queens. Staten Island was out of the question, and he didn't feel safe at his brother's place in Williamsburg. Ana invited Jamel to move in with her, and he did. Their dirty little secret was now out in the open.

Jamel took a pull from the coke-laced weed. High out of his mind, he sat naked on her couch, his legs spread. Ana engulfed his dick with her mouth and took him all the way in. Curved over into his lap, her head bobbed back and forth, as she started sucking and licking, stroking and tickling.

Jamel enjoyed the best of both worlds—a good blowjob and some great weed. His hand quickly went to her head. "Suck that dick! Ooooh yeah! Suck that dick!"

Ana worked his genitals like a pro. She cupped his balls while thrusting her mouth as far forward as she could go.

A display of fireworks exploded behind Jamel's eyes as they shut tight and his dick exploded deep into the back of her throat. He twitched with the last spurts of his seed into her mouth as she sucked and licked up the last of it. He looked down at her as she stared up at him. She made him forget about last week's violent episode with his brother and everyone else. The laced weed had Jamel feeling extraordinary. His cock was still raging hard as he enjoyed the caress of her silky-smooth skin.

Ana took the blunt from his hand and took a few pulls herself. They both were high out of their minds.

Beefing with his brother had Jamel stressed. He was also becoming irritated with Ana. Sneaking around was one thing, but having all of his business with her come to light made him feel dirty. She was his sister, wasn't she?

And part of him blamed her for getting busted. When they got to the Staten Island house he would put his hand on a bible that she seduced him. He didn't even want to fuck, but she persisted. Did she want to get caught? Ana was a vengeful little cunt. He knew that for sure.

The drugs had him bugging out. He stood up from the couch and walked toward the window. He constantly kept looking outside, becoming somewhat paranoid. He thought everyone was coming after him, from his foes to Apple and Kamel. The slightest noise had him jumping up and reaching for his gun. He thought his brother was trying to kill him. He was ready to shoot first; he wasn't dying by the gun. Not him. He was going out peacefully in his seventies with a hot bitch giving him head.

He continued to pace the room naked and clutching a revolver, looking out the window every minute or two.

"They come then they come, but I got something for their asses," Jamel said to himself, aiming the revolver out the window.

The streets were dark and quiet. Fear took over the primitive part of his brain, locking him down into survival mode. *He felt that everyone was trying to rob him of his ability to live his life. Darkness was washing over him, sending him down the road to perdition.*

His fear wasn't going to shut him down; it was waking him up. In the grip of silent panic, his eyes were wild, his pupils dilated, his heart racing, and his brain was on fire.

"Survival of the fittest," he proclaimed. "Kill 'em all!"

Ana inhaled strongly and slouched against the couch. She watched

Jamel lose his mind, tripping and talking to himself. She was stressed herself too, but the high made her problems easier to absorb. After sucking his dick, she sat back with the blunt glued to her lips. Her pussy was tingling, but Jamel was too busy with his paranoia to fuck her correctly.

Her dream was to end up with Kamel, but he only saw her as his little sister. Ana had been secretly in love with him forever. She was jealous of Kola. She had the man Ana always wanted, and now she made it easier for Kola to have him. Ana felt that she needed to correct the situation.

She didn't want to lose him to a bitch like Kola. Her manipulative ways didn't work, so now it was time to take a more drastic approach. Jamel was fun, but Kamel was the man she always dreamt about. It was time to show Apple and Kola how crazy she really was.

She walked to her closet and pulled out Apple's red mink coat that she had stolen the night of the fight and put it on. The red mink had her caramel skin glowing. She luxuriated in the expensive garment. It felt like butter gliding through her fingertips.

"Stupid bitches," she remarked. Ana vowed to make them both pay.

THIRTY-ONE

Mack D sat in the backseat of his Maybach and puffed on his cigar. The streets were calm for now. Too quiet. Maybe it was the calm before the storm. His product wasn't the strongest. The streets were complaining that it was inferior to the others. He was relying on the connection to be made with Eduardo. The Colombians produced some of the purest cocaine, and Eduardo was known to have the best. To be the best, Mack D needed to have the best.

The night was cold. The temperature was below twenty degrees, and light snow was in the forecast. Mack D patiently waited for the detectives to show up. He was warm and comfortable. After his cigar, he was going to pour himself a glass of cognac. He was paying for something valuable.

Several minutes later a black Ford Taurus pulled in front of his Maybach. Mack D watched the vehicle park. The driver's door opened up, and Detective Mogen stepped out. He was alone. He was in a long overcoat, his shoes shining and his Glock holstered beneath his coat.

Mack D unlocked the door, and Mogen slid inside from the bitter cold. "Shit! It's fuckin' cold!" He blew into his hands to create warmth.

Mack D said, "I'm not paying you for the weather update, Detective. Do you have what I asked for?"

He nodded and removed a folder from underneath his coat. He placed it into Mack D's hand. Mack D opened it and saw it had all the information he needed. Mack D paid him his $15,000.

Detective Mogen smiled. "It's always a pleasure doing business. Everything cool?"

"It is. You may leave now."

The detective nodded and exited the vehicle.

Mack D started looking through the information. It was the file on his daughter's death. Nichols. He went through page after page meticulously. He read the full report about her murder, and how she was killed.

Recently, one of his goons had hit pay dirt when he received information through the grapevine that Apple was responsible for Nichols' death. The streets spoke, and Mack D was hearing Apple had owed a debt to a loan shark, so they went after Nichols to clear her debt.

Seeing that no one knew Nichols was his daughter while he was locked up, he didn't hear any chatter. So he was left in the dark. The only thing Mack D received while he was incarcerated was a letter from Denise alleging that Nichols was running around being grown and she had gotten herself snatched up and killed. He was crushed. Someone had murdered his little girl, and he wasn't able to avenge her death.

Kola's stories about her and Apple's past and the vague explanations regarding Denise's and Nichols' murders had him intrigued. He suspected that Kola was leaving out specific details, so he paid to have the gaps filled in.

In the police report a few names were mentioned, but they were all dead.

However, the person that was truly responsible was still alive and free. Mack D felt Apple had gotten away with murder for too long. Now she needed to die. And if Kola didn't give him Eduardo, then she needed to die too.

THIRTY-TWO

Christmas was only a few weeks away, but Kola couldn't get in the holiday spirit. Though she had Sophia and Eduardo Jr. still in her home, she missed Peaches a lot, and even Apple. Things weren't the same without her niece around. The siblings missed Peaches too.

Her relationship with Kamel was stronger than ever, but the fear of losing him to either Mack D or Eduardo was stronger. Now that Jamel was at odds with Kamel, Jamel was even more unpredictable. Kola knew Jamel was getting high and killing people like there was no tomorrow. He was creating more enemies that Kamel would have to deal with.

Kola had too many things to worry about.

Mack D was constantly calling. Kola knew she couldn't keep ignoring him forever, so she finally answered his call. It'd been a moment. She thought he would be perturbed, but he wasn't. He was cordial and had an upbeat merriness to his voice.

"Kola, please, don't ever ignore my calls again. I was so worried. I thought something happened."

"Well, I'm fine," she replied, coldly.

"Good to hear. And regarding that Eduardo business, let's put it behind us for now. I see you're uncomfortable with that arrangement, so I won't push it. Okay?"

"I'm not uncomfortable with anything. I spoke with him and he doesn't want to do business with you now. But he claims he's coming home soon and he'll meet with you in person." Kola was making up the story as she went along.

"He's getting out of his Colombian prison soon? Really?"

"That's what he said."

"That easy."

"All it takes is money. He got me out, didn't he?"

"He did."

"Well he's coming home soon to take care of his family, and all those who pose a threat to his family will be dealt with."

Mack D chuckled. "Of course they will be. In any event, I want you and Apple to come and have a holiday dinner with me and my mother. I told her all about my two daughters, Nichols' sisters, and she wants to meet you girls."

"Where?"

"Lincoln projects."

"Why the projects?" Kola asked.

"Because that's where she lives. She refuses to move. Anyway, my mother wants to see her grandchildren," he replied.

Kola couldn't believe what she was hearing. Was he really serious? "Her grandchildren?" she uttered in disbelief.

"I miss you, Kola. It's been a moment since we saw each other and spoke. It's the holiday season. Let bygones be bygones."

Kola really hated what he represented. How could a rich man like him still have his mother living in the projects when he had the money to move her out?

She promised to meet with him. She also promised Mack D that she would bring Apple with her. He'd sternly requested her presence.

"Kola, don't come if you can't bring Apple."

"I said she'll come, but why is her presence so important?"

"Honestly, because she keeps refusing to come. I want to look her in the eye and tell her our beef is dead. I want to show her that I've changed and that she can trust me. So, you can bring her? And before you say yes just to get me off the phone, I want to go Christmas shopping and buy y'all something nice. What does Apple like?"

"Apple?"

"Yes, Apple. And I mean something big. Car, jewelry, money in a box with a bow."

"Shit, well since you're playing Santa, what about me?"

"I already know what my favorite twin likes. Don't worry. It'll blow your mind."

Kola tossed her eyes in the air. "Apple likes what I like. We're twins, remember? And she'll be grateful for whatever you buy her."

Mack D promised it was going to be one big happy family gathering.

"And, Kola."

"Yes?"

"Wear the purple mink I gifted you. Have Apple wear the red one."

"I'll wear mine, but you should know by now that nobody can make Apple do anything."

"You better start making Apple do as I say, or I will."

THIRTY-THREE

Tonight was the night. Either do or die. There was no turning back from what she had planned. The kids were at Ms. Kendricks' house, and Kamel was with Maleek taking care of business.

Kola donned the purple mink coat, climbed into a cab, and anticipated bloodshed with a powerful drug kingpin. She told the driver her destination then she sat back, exhaled, and prayed she would make it out of the lion's den alive and with the lion's head. Tonight, Mack D had to die.

An hour later, Kola climbed out of the cab in Harlem. She was back at Lincoln Projects. It was cold, and the area looked barren. The hustlers and fiends were probably hibernating from the bitter wind that ripped through the night. Being back in Harlem brought back memories.

She looked around and sighed. It was now or never. She had her .380 and a blade on her, but was that enough?

Kola walked toward the building Mack D's mother was residing in unaware that someone had been following her. The assailant strutted her way in a luxurious coat, head hung low. The fur hood was over her head, masking her face, and she gripped a .45. She wanted to kill Kola. She was seething with jealousy and envy and anxious to put a bullet in Kola's head. Being high off that Colombian white didn't help the situation.

Kola walked ahead, her eyes focused on the lobby. The assailant hurried behind her and was about to raise the pistol and fire.

Then, suddenly, she heard a deep, baritone voice shout, "Apple!"—and then the shot happened—*Boom! It* exploded like dynamite. The gunshot cracked into the air as loud as thunder but without the raw power of a storm.

It startled Kola. She spun around and was face to face with the barrel of a large still-smoking Desert Eagle. She stood wide-eyed and was shocked to see a body lying face down, draped under a red mink coat with a bullet to the back of the head.

The assailant let off two more rounds. *Boom! Boom!*

Kola couldn't even scream. She couldn't react. The hitman had her strangled with fear, as she caught him murdering her sister dead to rights.

"Burn in hell, Apple," were his parting words.

The man's cold, black eyes locked into Kola, and then he lowered the gun from her head and hurried away.

Kola almost collapsed. Finally she ran to her sister with a gush of emotions taking over her body. Tears streamed down her face, and her body shook violently. What the fuck was she doing here! she thought. She looked at the body and realized it wasn't Apple but Ana. Ana? The myriad of feelings that she just felt came to an abrupt holt. It fucked her mind up that she didn't know what was going on.

As the police sirens blared in the distance, Kola fled from the crime scene before the cops showed up. She couldn't think straight, but she knew one thing for sure—it was definitely an organized hit on her sister, but they'd fucked up. She had a hunch who was behind it, but she wasn't sure.

The farther she moved herself away from the murder, the more she collected herself. Whoever it was, they thought her sister was dead.

She pulled out her cell phone and called Mack D, screaming, "Someone killed Apple!"

To her surprise, Mack D calmly stated, "It had to be done."

"What?" she yelled, putting on an award-winning performance. "You knew about this? This was you!"

"You disappointed me, Kola. But I say this—Nichols." He hung up abruptly.

Kola's plan was destroyed, but the good news was he believed Apple was dead. Somehow she felt she could use this to her advantage.

Mack D smiled at what he'd pulled off. He wanted to see Kola sweat. He wanted to see the fear in her eyes. He wanted to toy with her. He wanted to slowly torture her. However, he still needed her to make the connection with Eduardo; it was the only reason why she was still alive.

While the murder was happening at the projects, Mack D was at one of his stash houses with all of his goons plotting his next move. He was holding court when he got the call about the hit.

"It's done," the killer said via cell phone.

Mack D nodded and smiled. "Stupid bitches," he said.

Richard was on standby though to do the real dirty work. He was itching to get his hands dirty and execute what he did best, murder. Standing on the sidelines and watching didn't suit him. Richard wanted to kill every last one of them. He wanted to avenge Damien's death more than his own father. His boss wanted to play this cat-and-mouse game. He didn't understand. He wasn't pleased.

"I think keeping her alive can become a problem," one of Mack D's lieutenants stated about Kola.

Richard agreed. "You should have killed her too, and let me hunt down the brothers."

"That connection is valuable. With quality cocaine like that, our profits will triple, and our influence will grow so far west, my brothers, our blood will bleed green." Mack D took a pull from his cigar then added, "Killing Apple will get that bitch to weaken, and she will want to make the connection happen. Besides, she wanted her sister dead a few years ago. I only finished what she started."

"If she truly wanted her sister dead, then she would have been dead. Kola was the main bitch of the FBI's most wanted cartel lord. Obviously, there is a sisterly bond that trumps all beef. I feel it's foolish, Mack," Richard chimed.

"Believe me, it is not foolish, Richard. I thought this through. We leave her naked on these streets—no protection at all—and she'll come running to daddy." Mack D looked at his prized killer and said, "Go hunt, my friend. I want the brothers dead too. *Now*."

"I'm on it," Richard replied.

Mack D sat in his chair and continued smoking his cigar, feeling like the world revolved around him.

THIRTY-FOUR

K ola called Kamel immediately to tell him what happened. "Ana's dead!" she exclaimed into the phone.

"What?" Kamel was shocked.

She couldn't give Kamel the reason why Ana was in the projects following her, but she knew Ana was up to no good, and it'd cost her her life.

"Mack D put a hit out on Apple. We gotta find her and keep her safe!"

Kamel was profoundly concerned about Kola's well-being. He asked her numerous questions. Kola had to come clean with him. She admitted that she was meeting with Mack D behind his back.

He was furious. He snarled more than spoke. Anger boiled deep in his system, as hot as lava. His little sister was dead, and Kola was linking up with Mack D. He didn't know what to think. The pressure of this raging sea of anger he felt made him say things he didn't mean.

Kamel was worried sick, but he had to keep his mind right and think. He hurried home and got the kids from Ms. Kendricks. Things needed to change. He wondered if their safety and security had been put in jeopardy. Were they still safe in Staten Island?

"You need to call Jamel," she said. "You need to warn him."

Kamel knew she was right. They hadn't spoken in a while. He was still upset with Jamel for deceiving Kola into having sex with him, and then taking advantage of Ana and having sex with her. He was disgusted with his brother. But no matter how disgusted and upset he was with Jamel, he didn't want him murdered.

Kamel called his brother's cell phone, and after several rings, Jamel finally picked up. His brother's voice sounded groggy.

Kamel didn't hold back or sugarcoat anything. "Yo, Ana's dead."

"What! What the fuck you talkin' about, Twin?"

"Something happened. It was a botched hit on Apple."

"Mack D?" Jamel asked.

"Yeah."

"I'm gonna kill that muthafucka! Yo, I swear, he's dead! He's fuckin' dead!" Jamel shouted.

"You need to chill out, Jamel, and think."

"Nah, fuck that! Fuck that! Aaaaaaaaaaaaahhh! I don't need to think about shit! Ana's dead. I ain't hearing shit you gotta say, Kamel! I'm gonna hunt that nigga down and take him out. And you know what? After I take him out, I'm takin' that bitch Kola out, because I know it's her fault. She ain't never liked Ana anyway."

"What! You definitely need to chill out. You're talking crazy, nigga," Kamel spat.

"Fuck that!"

"No, fuck you! And relax!"

Jamel didn't want to relax or think about things. He hung up on his brother. He was ready to react off of impulse. He was devastated. Ana's murder set him off, and he was like TNT with a short fuse. It gave him the excuse he needed to take things to the next level.

Kamel tried to call his brother back repeatedly, but Jamel refused to pick up. He was done talking. Kamel had no choice but to call Kola and warn her about the threat. He didn't want to take any chances. They had to make moves and make them fast.

THIRTY-FIVE

Kola rushed toward the city and into the Marriott in midtown Manhattan, where Apple was staying with Peaches. They had Maleek keeping tabs on them and the hotel, making sure they were safe. Kola missed Peaches a great deal. Her niece was always on her mind. Apple too. Kola once read: "The weak can never forgive; forgiveness is an attribute of the strong." Kola knew she was a strong woman. She'd forgiven Apple plenty of times.

Kola marched toward the front desk and pretended to be Apple, saying she'd lost her keys. The receptionist was about to give Kola another key when unexpectedly her supervisor decided to follow protocol and ask Kola for ID.

"I left it in the room," Kola said.

The receptionist was told to escort Kola to her room and verify the ID.

Kola and the young girl took the elevator to the sixth floor and then walked toward the room number. The receptionist used her keycard to enter the room. Kola was on alert, her hand subtly inside her purse around the handle of her .380.

The receptionist turned around and expected Kola to retrieve her ID. She was waiting.

Kola smiled and put five hundred dollars in her hand. "This is for you. A small incentive, because you do remember me, right?" Kola said.

The receptionist looked at her and suddenly remembered, "Yes, I do." She greedily took the money and left.

No one was inside the room, but Kola knew Apple was still staying there. It looked lived in. Her and Peaches' clothes were everywhere.

Kola took a seat on the bed and lay across it. She was tired. She ended up falling asleep.

❦

Two hours later, Kola was awakened with a gun in her face. At first she was startled, but it was Apple, and she was confident that her sister wasn't going to execute her in a hotel room.

She pushed the gun from out of her face and sat up.

"What are you doing here?" Apple asked.

"I came to see you."

Apple frowned, but she didn't act up, especially not with Peaches sleeping in the next bed. It was late, and Peaches was tired and had fallen asleep in her mother's arms as she carried her into the hotel.

Kola smiled at her sleeping niece. "I miss her," she said.

"What do you want, Kola?" Apple asked.

"We need to talk."

"About what?"

"Ana's dead."

The news surprised Apple. "Kola that's fucked up."

"I know."

"How?"

"It was a hit. I'm assuming Mack D's goons thought she was you."

"Me? Why would they think that?"

"Most likely because she was wearing the coat Mack D bought you."

"My coat? That little thief." Apple was furious. "I told you not to trust him."

"I know. It was a mistake."

"It was a mistake that could have cost us both our lives."

"You're right. He thinks you're dead, so that makes you and Peaches safe," Kola said.

"We will never be safe if Mack D's alive."

"Tonight I had a plan that will no longer work. Mack D will have his guard up around me. We may have to flee today to fight tomorrow."

"I can't keep running, Kola. Damn. This ain't even our beef."

"We don't have any other options."

Kola went on to tell Apple the details about Ana's murder and the fact that Ana had followed her to try to kill her.

Apple was saddened by the news. Ana was a manipulative bitch. Still, Apple felt she didn't deserve to die in her place. That was fucked up.

Kola told her side of the story about her episode with Jamel. She told Apple the truth of how he tricked her into having sex with him.

Apple was sickened by Jamel's transgressions. She knew every word was true.

Their conversation transitioned into Eduardo. Kola just couldn't let it go. She stared at her sister and said, "Be honest with me, and tell me what happened between you and Eduardo. Did he rape you?"

Apple shook her head no. She admitted that Eduardo gave her an opportunity that she couldn't turn down. Colombia was never her town— Apple never felt comfortable or welcome there. She was aching to return to the States. Eduardo was able to make it possible. She needed to find her daughter.

Kola immediately forgave Apple, knowing she would have done the same thing for her child.

As for Eduardo, Kola knew she would never forgive him. The thought that he had again fucked two sisters, sickened her to her core.

THIRTY-SIX

Y ou need me to come with you?" Maleek asked Kamel.

"Nah, I'm good. I need to talk to him alone."

Maleek nodded. Kamel was the boss, but Maleek didn't trust anyone, not even Jamel. He was always cautious and ready to protect Kamel even if it meant his own life.

Kamel stepped out of the Yukon armed with a 9 mm tucked in his waistband and clad in a snuggly North Face winter coat. They were parked in the lot of the closed amusement park on W15th Street in Coney Island, Brooklyn, a stone's throw from the boardwalk.

The cold licked at Kamel's face and crept under his clothes, spreading across his skin like the icy tide on a winter beach. He wrapped his coat around him tighter and walked toward the boardwalk. What residual heat he had absorbed in the truck was gone. He was stunned to see his brother on the boardwalk wearing only jeans, a T-shirt, and a Yankees fitted.

"What the fuck!" Kamel muttered, staring at his brother's insanity.

Jamel was facing the ocean, smoking a cigarette coolly like it was warm weather. He turned around to see Kamel approaching.

Kamel already knew his brother wasn't in his right mind. "You ain't cold, nigga?" Kamel asked.

"Fuck that shit! I'm ready to kill 'em all, Kamel, fo' real. They murdered Ana. She was family, nigga. What you gonna do about it?"

"We need to think this through."

"Fuck thinking shit through. You know what? You fuckin' changed on me, Twin. You been soft ever since that bitch came into your life."

"You high, nigga. Watch your mouth."

"Or what, nigga? What the fuck you gon' do? We at war out there, so there's no fuckin' negotiation, no thinking shit through. Just bloodshed, nigga. I'm ready to fuckin' murder these niggas!" Jamel shouted.

Kamel stared at his brother pacing back and forth, looking like a madman.

Jamel wanted to know the details of Ana's death, but Kamel was vague with the information. He took one final drag from his cigarette and flicked it into the cold sand. "It's all my fault, nigga. It's my fault." Jamel felt guilty. He felt he should have been there to protect Ana. He allowed the animals to get to her.

Kamel looked into his eyes. They were a bottomless pool of darkness, death, violence, sorrow, and pain. He couldn't see the whites of his eyes nor the vessels that flowed through them. Jamel had lost his soul a long time ago.

"What you're talking about? What's your fault?"

Jamel wiped his face free of some invisible dirt—he was visibly tweaking. He couldn't keep still. He stared at Kamel and said, "I fucked up a long time ago, Twin."

"What you mean? What did you do?" Kamel asked.

"It's because of me that Ana's pops was killed."

"What?" Kamel was confused.

Rocky was like an uncle to Jamel and Kamel. He was a thorough dude who ran a fierce crew. Rocky was well-respected and was in the streets every day, making money hand over fist. Rocky was close to the twins and their father, a natural-born hustler named Cannon, who was like a brother to Rocky. Together, Cannon and Rocky once ruled the streets with an iron fist. Rocky and the twins' father always had each other's back and trusted each other.

One day, someone had the audacity to murder Rocky. He was gunned down in his home. The streets suspected it was a setup. The fingers pointed toward someone close to him—someone he trusted. Cannon's name continually came up. Rocky's crew suspected betrayal.

Two months later, Rocky's crew murdered Cannon.

Jamel and Kamel were devastated. Their father was gone, and the man they looked up to as an uncle was gone too. It was chaos, and subsequently the twins were targeted.

Guns blazed into the night, more men died, but the twins survived the deadly ordeal. Kamel swore he would kill the men responsible for his father and uncle's murders.

Ana was the only family they had left. They protected her and took care of her. They considered her to be their little sister.

"I killed Rocky."

"Rocky? Why?"

Jamel went into detail, admitting that years ago, he and his friend were the ones who'd murdered Rocky when Ana was only eleven years old. He was nineteen at the time and he needed a come-up. Jamel knew that if he robbed Rocky that he would have to kill him. Ana's dad was an OG, and he wouldn't have stopped until he found the men that robbed him. It was how Jamel got his seed money for a few kilos.

Kamel was stunned silent by the news.

Then Jamel added, "I lied to you too. I did kill PJ. I shot that nigga and stuffed him into the trunk of his car. I was tired of him laying hands on Ana."

The news was profoundly unacceptable to Kamel. Jamel was psychotic. There was no doubt about it. Kamel glared at him, and he couldn't help himself. He swung suddenly, punching him and knocking him on his ass.

"You stupid muthafucka!" he shouted. "You know what you did? Your greed and stupidity got our father killed."

"I know what I did. I had to do it to survive and get us hooked up. If it wasn't for me, where'd you be, nigga? Huh? Nowhere! I started this shit. I had the fuckin' balls to do what needed doing."

Kamel knew his brother was off—way off! There was no coming back for him. Jamel was deep in the abyss of evil and destruction. Kamel felt that not only Kola's life was in eminent danger, but so were his and possibly the kids'. There and now, he knew he needed to leave the city.

THIRTY-SEVEN

The naked winter trees lined the avenue. It was another cold New York day. Detective Mogen and Lowell's breaths ascended in visible clouds.

The detectives walked toward the dark Impala talking and laughing, their pockets lined with ten thousand dollars each. They'd delivered the information for each man in the photos to Mack D. It was only business on their end. Both cops yearned for an early retirement.

Lowell said, "I got my eyes on this boat—a Boston Whaler. It's a beauty."

"Not too long until you're fishing in the deep sea forgetting about this place here."

"I already got my fishing poles lined up and ready to catch me some red snappers and catfish. I can already taste them."

The men laughed.

As they were about to climb inside the Impala, swiftly a hooded thug carrying a large automatic appeared out of nowhere. He lifted the gun to Mogen and shot him in the face at point-blank range.

Mogen coiled over and dropped to the ground, dead.

Shocked and frightened, Detective Lowell desperately tried to remove his holstered Glock, but the hooded thug was already upon him, blasting six shots into the detective and killing him instantly.

Satisfied, Jamel hurried to the idling BMW, where Mark-Mark was behind the wheel. He pulled his hood back and smiled. "Fuck Mack D! I'm killing all his people!"

Mark-Mark walked into his building lobby a week after his involvement in the gunning down of Detectives Lowell and Mogen. The streets were hot. The murders were front-page news. The story had come out about them being corrupt and working for a murderous drug kingpin. It was the hot topic.

Mark-Mark stepped into the elevator and pushed his floor. As the elevator ascended, he pulled out a blunt and sparked up. Blunts were like cigarettes to him. He was armed with two guns. He was always on alert, knowing that anyone connected to Jamel was a target.

Jamel was on a warpath, killing everything that moved. It came to light that he'd persuaded three of Mack D's men to rob him, and then he and his crew stole from them. His deal with the Armenians was falling apart. He wasn't getting the one million fast enough.

Mark-Mark took a drag from his blunt. The elevator doors opened, and before he could take a single step, a loud shotgun blast violently lifted him off his feet and slammed him into the wall so hard, he was dead before he hit the ground. He lay ripped open in a pool of his own blood.

Richard stood over the body and frowned. He didn't say a word. He pivoted and coolly walked away.

Mike was too paranoid to leave his Brooklyn apartment. He'd heard about the murders of the cops, knowing Jamel was implicated in that mess. And then he heard about Mark-Mark's gruesome demise. Mark-

Mark was a careful and tough white boy, so he knew whoever had gotten to him was a straight professional.

Mike refused to answer his phone or step outside. If he was hungry, then he ordered takeout, and when the deliveryman came to the door, he would slide the money underneath the door and tell them to leave the food in the hallway. Only when he was certain they were gone, would he open his door and get his meal.

He regularly carried his snub-nose revolver and a Glock with him everywhere and always kept a round in the chamber. He kept his windows closed, making his apartment always dark. He knew either the cops were going to raid his apartment, or niggas were ready to kill him, and he wasn't about to make it easier for either one.

Mike sat watching TV in the living room, an old episode of *Diff'rent Strokes*, laughing at Arnold's antics. The gun was on his lap. He was waiting for his Chinese food order to come.

An hour later someone was knocking at his door. He got up with the revolver gripped in his fist.

"Who?" he asked.

"You ordered Chinese?"

"Yeah, leave that shit by the door." Mike slid a twenty-dollar bill underneath the doorway. "Keep the change."

"Thank you," the delivery man replied. He walked away.

Mike looked through the peephole to make sure everything was safe and clear. When he was satisfied, he unlocked the door and quickly collected his food. But the minute he closed his door Mike felt a sudden and unwanted presence behind him. It gave him a chill.

He turned suddenly to try and strike with his gun, but he was too slow. Richard sharply grabbed him into a tight choke hold and thrust the sharp, six-inch blade into his temple. Mike squirmed in Richard's arms, dying slowly.

Richard held him up until the lights in his eyes darkened for good. Mike's body went lifeless in Richard's crushing arms, and Richard released him. Mike's body dropped to the floor. Richard looked down at him, unsmiling. Murder got his blood boiling; it made him alive. The main prizes—Kamel and Jamel—were last on his list. They couldn't run or hide from him. He was going to permanently put their lights out.

First Mark-Mark, then Mike, and now Dennis and Bird were found slaughtered in the Hudson River, their bodies frozen from the cold. Their throats were slashed so deeply, their heads were almost severed. Jamel knew he was next if he didn't react first. His crew had been wiped out. He was now on the run. Mack D had whispered to the police that Jamel was responsible for the corrupt cops' murders, and an APB went out that he was a man of interest in a police shooting.

Jamel felt that he was no longer safe in Brooklyn, Queens, or Harlem. He decided he would hide out in Staten Island then make his way farther South, maybe Georgia then Florida— keep a low profile until the heat blew over. He missed Kamel and Apple. It'd been weeks since he'd seen them.

He spent his time getting high off cocaine and weed. He planned on not going out without a fight. He was ready for them when they came. He constantly wore Kevlar and armed himself with guns and knives from head to toe.

He stepped out of Ana's Queens home, his eyes dancing everywhere. He was bold and ready, itching to kill anyone that came his way. He walked toward his car parked in the driveway and openly carried two fully loaded 9 mm's. Every minute mattered. He didn't trust anyone.

He hit the alarm to the Benz, unlocking the doors. He checked the backseat and looked around his surrounding area, and everything seemed normal.

But Jamel was extra paranoid. And he had the right to be.

As he was about to get in his car to head to Staten Island, he immediately saw the threat via the window—his reflection gave him away. Richard's large Desert Eagle was pointed at the back of Jamel's head.

Jamel didn't freeze up. He dove to the ground, and the shots rang out but missed him barely, and the window on the driver's side exploded. Jamel spun around and returned fire at Richard. His two 9 mm's exploded, pushing Richard off his feet and tumbling him to the grass. Richard was on his back, looking lifeless.

Jamel wasn't sure if he was dead or not. He crouched and cautiously moved toward the body, ready to finish it, but Richard had a surprise waiting.

A single shot ripped through Jamel's side, and he dropped to his knee, wincing from the pain.

Another shooter came from behind, but he missed the kill shot.

Jamel spun and shot the man in the head then he turned around just in time to see Richard standing up and pointing his gun at him, and he fired at Richard. Two shots went off simultaneously from both guns, but only one did its job.

Richard was shocked that he got hit in the chest. The blood seeped through his clothing. He glared at Jamel cursing, and then fell dead.

Jamel refused to stick around. He'd just murdered Mack D's number one killer. The bounty was about to triple on his head. He jumped into his Benz and sped off. He was on his way to Staten Island.

The house was empty. Kamel made sure of that. There were no children laughing or playing in the backyard or in the house, his woman's sweet voice was absent from the residence. There was only silence from room to room. There was absolute stillness. Not a sound could be heard either close at hand or in the far distance. It was an eerie sort of tranquility.

Kamel felt the home in Staten Island was no longer safe. He, Kola, Apple, and the kids all felt like prisoners. So he got his family away from there and had them staying at a hotel in New Jersey, where Maleek was protecting them.

The following day they all had a long flight to Santa Cruz, California. They planned on leaving New York for good. They felt that the West Coast was far enough from Mack D's violent reach. With Kamel's money, they could start over and probably live comfortably.

But Eduardo was a different story.

Kamel gathered the last of his belongings from the house. He had everything he needed. He looked around one last time and was about to exit when he saw Jamel's Benz coming to a stop in the driveway.

He kept his hand near his weapon, his attention on Jamel storming out of the Benz and hurrying to the front porch. He was bleeding.

Jamel came flying into the house and was met with Kamel glaring at him with a Glock in his hand.

Jamel was out of breath and staggering. He fell into the wall and collapsed to the ground, exclaiming, "Bro, I need help!"

"What the fuck, Jamel! What happened?"

"I got that muthafucka! He came at me, and I got that nigga!"

"Who?"

"Richard—Mack D's boy. Fuck him!"

Kamel was shocked. He killed Richard; the streets didn't think it was possible for him to die. But from his brother's appearance it looked like he'd gotten into a fierce gun battle and barely won.

"Yo, we are one step away from killing that sonofabitch, Twin. His right hand has gone down, and he's weak. So now it's our turn," Jamel said breathlessly.

Kamel looked at his brother. They didn't have the same dreams. They were living two different lives. Kamel couldn't continue living dangerously and taking risks. He wanted to be a family man now. He wanted out of the game. He wanted to be left alone and love his woman.

Jamel stood up, holding his side. He looked at his brother and said, "I'm a'ight, bro, it's only a flesh wound. But we good now, nigga. We good. It's *our* time to shine."

They weren't good. They would never be good again. Kamel didn't want to shine in the underworld any more. He had lost his appetite for that lifestyle.

Jamel looked around the house. He suddenly noticed it was empty. No one was home.

"Where's everybody?" he asked.

"They're gone, Jamel."

"Gone? Where?"

"Far from here."

"What you mean, nigga?"

"I mean, we done with this life for good. We're leaving New York, all of us," Kamel informed him.

Jamel looked at his brother. "You tryin' to leave me, Twin? That bitch is tryin' to take you away from me. Nah, I won't let her!"

"Nigga, it ain't your call. It's my call, and I said I'm done with this. I'm done with us!" Kamel exclaimed. "Look at you, you're fucked up, nigga—getting high, killing everything that moves and thinking you gonna live through this shit. Nigga, you're doing one hundred miles an hour on a dark, slippery street, and you're about to lose control and hit a brick wall. Think, Jamel, think!"

Jamel felt dejected. Every word from his brother stung, only fueling the fire that burned inside of him. His fingers and jaw began to clench.

"Where the fuck you gonna go, nigga? This is all we know."

"No, this is all that you want to know, not me. I got a family now. I got other dreams I wanna see come true."

"Family? I thought I was your family," Jamel said sadly.

"I love you, Jamel, and you will always be my family, but look at you—look at what you're becoming. Ana's dead, your crew's dead, you killed two cops, and now you're on the run, and you warring with Mack D. How you think this is going to end for you?"

"Nigga, fuck you then! I don't fuckin' need you, nigga. I'm good. You know why, Kamel? Because I'm a fuckin' survivor. I came this far, and I'm a fuckin' warrior," he announced, pounding his chest with his fist, his eyes burning into his brother.

Kamel stared at his brother and he felt sorry for him. He had no one. Apple was leaving with them. Ana was dead. He simply had his pain and his violence.

"Leave, nigga. Go on and be The Brady Bunch wit' that bitch and them kids. But how long you think it's gonna last, nigga? You think you Mike Brady, muthafucka? Like you ain't did your dirt and kill niggas. Now you wanna switch up and shit, get all sanctified and shit. Fuck you! You ain't family, nigga!" Jamel exclaimed loud and clear.

Kamel had no words for Jamel. He was done talking.

Jamel paced around the room, amped up. He pulled out a cocaine-laced blunt from his pocket and lit up right there. He took a few pulls and blew smoke in Kamel's direction.

"Family." Jamel laughed. "Let's see how long your family last when your true colors come out. Nigga, where you gon' go? You ain't safe nowhere, bro. And you know what? I'm gonna find them bitches, Apple and Kola, and guess what I'm gon' do to them? I'm gonna show them my true colors. Yeah, nigga, they taking you away from me, so I'm gonna take them away from you."

"You need help."

"I don't need a damn thing, not from you or anyone. Fuck outta here, nigga! Run nigga, run," Jamel said, mocking him.

Jamel turned and looked out the window, smoking his blunt and turning his back on his brother, indicating Kamel was a foul nigga to walk out on his own flesh and blood.

Kamel was hurt by his brother's words and his appearance. He knew the inevitable was coming for him, death or incarceration. Tears trickled down his face as he stared at him. He didn't want to see any harm come to Jamel, but he knew Mack D was going to find him and torture him to death.

Kamel walked behind his brother and said, "I love you, Jamel. I always will." He raised the gun to the back of Jamel's head and pulled the trigger.

Boom!

The bullet propelled Jamel forward into the window, and he dropped dead by his brother's feet.

Kamel's tears continued to fall. It was the hardest decision he'd ever made, but he felt it had to be done. It was either by him or the streets. Kamel knew that Jamel would not have rested until he killed his happiness.

He dried his tears and left the body there, hoping his brother would be found soon.

Killing Jamel closed that chapter of his life, and he was ready to start a new one. His next move was risky and damn near suicidal, but he was ready to die for Kola. He was tired of her running and being scared. It had to end. He was ready to confront the man she feared and talk to him man to man.

THIRTY-EIGHT

While her family was trying to enjoy a new life in Santa Cruz, Kola's plane was landing at El Dorado International Airport in Bogotá, Colombia. Today was judgment day for her. She planned on visiting Eduardo in jail. She wanted to talk to him face to face and, if she had to, beg for his mercy. It worked once. Could it possibly work again?

Kola's stomach shifted uneasily. She pinched her nails into her skin. She couldn't relax or think straight.

Eduardo knew she was coming. They spoke briefly, and he didn't sound too pleased with her. Kola worried about the outcome. No matter where she moved to, the thought of him finding her would forever be entrenched in her mind. How could she live like that, watching over her shoulder, nervously waiting for the inevitable to happen?

She stepped off the plane looking sexy in a pair of white pants, expensive heels, a tank top that hugged her so fierce, it was like part of her skin, and expensive Chanel shades. Her hair was now short, like Toni Braxton's back in the day, and she didn't wear any makeup.

The minute she stepped off the plane and into the terminal, she was met by two of Eduardo's underlings. They were mean and dirty. They hurriedly whisked her away to their Jeep Wrangler and drove her to La Modelo prison. It was a lengthy ride, and Kola's stomach was doing flips. She was back on Colombian soil, and anything could happen to her.

The Wrangler came to a stop. From the outside, the prison looked like a fierce and dirty place. Inside, it was hell on earth, with over 10,000 inmates. In 2000, twenty-five prisoners were murdered in a riot.

The prison was a haunting reminder for Kola of her short stay at the woman's prison there. It was a place she wanted to forget. She was escorted from the jeep and escorted inside the prison. She was flanked by Eduardo's goons, who protected her from the perverts that leered. The men howled, gawked, whistled, and even flashed their dicks at her. The many lustful stares aimed at Kola made her feel naked. But they knew to not touch her. She was protected. She belonged to Eduardo.

Kola said a prayer. She didn't know if it would work or not, but she hoped for a miracle. She was hoping this trip wouldn't be her last. The thugs escorted her deeper into the reeking, overcrowded prison, where the predators fed on the weak.

They guided her toward a lone room at the end of a long corridor. The door opened, and Kola was pushed inside. It was bright inside, and the concrete walls were a thick grey. No windows, one way in, and one way out. There was a small table and two chairs on opposite ends.

Kola stood there alone anticipating the worst. She refused to take a seat. She felt more comfortable standing.

Several minutes went by before the door opened up and Eduardo loomed into the room.

Kola gasped seeing him again. There he was, standing right in front of her, in the flesh, his expression cold. He was well groomed and wearing a beige linen shirt and slacks. He looked like he was at a resort rather than a prison hellhole.

"You cut your hair," he said.

"A new look, a different me. You look good, Eduardo. How you been in here?"

He stood near the door and gazed at her. He didn't answer her question.

Kola felt uneasy. She tried to breathe easy, to not look nervous. She was a gangster and had been through gun battles and war. She had held her own in the streets for a long time, but standing in front of Eduardo, one of the most powerful men in the world, she felt uncomfortable.

"Sit," he said. "Let's talk."

Kola took a seat at the table, and Eduardo did the same. She looked at him and said, "I never meant to hurt you."

"But you did."

"Eduardo, I loved you."

"And I loved you, but you betrayed me."

"Betrayed you? I did nothing but been loyal to you. I took your kids to America liked you asked, and I'm taking very good care of them. I was a loyal and faithful woman to you when I came to this country, but you hurt me with your whores and your disrespect."

"Do you love him more than me?" Eduardo asked.

Kola did. It was hard to look Eduardo in his eyes because her eyes quickly revealed what her heart was feeling.

"I love him, Eduardo, and I do want to marry him. But I don't want to be looking over my shoulders for the rest of my life. I don't want any repercussions from you."

"You know you're a foolish girl, Kola. Do you remember our promise?"

"I do."

"You broke our promise, Kola. You were supposed to be mine forever."

"How, Eduardo, with you in here? You let me leave for America for a reason, and I'm asking you please, in your heart, to let me go, to forgive me and Kamel. He's a good man, and he doesn't deserve to die over something I did. I never wanted this to happen, and I never disrespected you. I always have been straight up with you, Eduardo. I just want us to be happy. That's all I want from you."

Eduardo didn't say a word at first. His eyes locked into her.

Then he said, "I'll give you your freedom, Kola. But look me in my eyes and tell me one thing—do you still love me?"

She was torn. Of course, she still loved him. She would always love him, but she was no longer in love with him. She looked Eduardo squarely in his eyes. "I love you, Eduardo, but I'm not in love with you anymore. I'm in love with Kamel. He's a great man, and he's good to your kids. Your kids, Eduardo. He treats them like they're his own."

Eduardo listened intently. He didn't show any emotions. With the snap of his fingers he could cause her death or keep her in Colombia and she would never see home again.

"You have my blessing, Kola."

She couldn't believe it. She was shocked. "What? Are you serious?"

"Yes."

She couldn't read him. Her heart was happy, but her mind was skeptical. It seemed too easy. Maybe he did have a change of heart, or maybe he had some kind of motive. It was scary not knowing.

"Why the blessing, Eduardo? I mean, I'm very thankful. But I need to be sure. I want to know if this is for real."

Eduardo stood up and said, "Leave, Kola, before I change my mind." He waved her off and dismissed her. He turned and left the room abruptly.

Kola couldn't ask any more questions. He gave her his word, but she felt uneasy. She slowly stood up and walked out of the room behind him, her heart pounding. She was met by the same goons that met her at the airport.

"You leave now," one of them said to her.

"Leave to go where?" she asked.

"Back home," he said.

Home sounded great to her. She followed them out of the prison and climbed back into the Jeep Wrangler. The men were silent and aloof. Her palms were sweaty, and her heart was beating like crazy.

Kola thought about the five million she had buried in the cemetery. She hadn't thought about how to go and retrieve the money herself and find some way to smuggle it into the U.S.

As they drove, the driver's cell phone rang. He answered.

Kola watched him. She knew she wasn't out of the frying pan yet.

It was a quick call. The driver nodded and hung up.

Kola noticed that they were driving in a different direction, away from the airport and deeper into the country.

"Where are we going?" she asked.

They ignored her. The jeep was doing seventy, so it would have been suicidal for her to jump out.

Thirty miles into the country, they stopped and dragged her out of the vehicle. She fought them rough and hard, kicking and screaming. She wasn't going out without a fight.

Eduardo had given his men the order to bury her, and they were about to carry out his order.

The area was isolated, far away from the road and people. She was driven to a kill sight where an unmarked grave was already dug.

Kola punched, scratched, and kicked, but she was knocked across the back of her head by a pistol and fell face-forward into the ground. She started to cry. She couldn't think or see straight. She didn't want to die in Colombia. She knew if they killed and buried her, her body would rot in the country, and she would be never found.

Kola continued fighting, though it looked bleak for her.

The thug hit her again, making her nose bleed.

The second man had her at gunpoint. He said to Kola, "*Puta*, make it easier on yourself and stop fighting. We will make it quick. We promise."

Kola refused to be killed like she was a nobody and have her body buried in the middle of nowhere. "Don't do this! Please, no! No! I got money. I can make y'all rich!" she yelled.

They both were stone-cold killers paid by Eduardo to kill her and dump the body. Everything she had to say was falling on deaf ears.

Kola continued yelling at them. "It's five million dollars. It's buried somewhere. I can take y'all to it. The money is all yours. It's in a cemetery. Please, just let me go! Let me live," she screamed out.

They looked at each other, but they still declined the offer. She could be lying, and Eduardo was a man they didn't want to cross.

Kola tried to stand and run, but they kicked her down into the dirt and punched her. Her white outfit now soiled.

"You don't run from us," the gunman growled.

She was near the hole. It was deep and dark. This was about to be her final resting place. On her knees and crying, Kola felt the barrel of his gun pressed to the back of her head. She was a dead woman, and there was no way out. She regretted coming to Colombia.

Her life started to flash before her eyes. She thought about Apple, Peaches, the siblings, her life growing up, and most importantly, she thought about Kamel. Her memories all came speeding through her head in one big blur. Kola knew she would be missed.

She closed her eyes and waited for the bang, her tears falling like a monsoon. She shivered and prayed to God.

The men towered over her had nothing but coldness in their eyes. It was time to execute her. Just as one of them was about to pull the trigger, his cell phone rang, and he answered, "Que?"

THIRTY-NINE

Kamel arrived an hour before Kola in Colombia, and he planned on meeting Eduardo face to face. Kamel had never seen a place like Colombia. It was different. It was poor, yet it was rich. The country was mountainous and so green. However he had no time to sightsee. He had to pull all his strings and call in favors, asking some of his own to get here— Bogotá. He had a connected friend arrange a meeting with Eduardo. It cost Kamel a lot of money, but he loved Kola and wanted to protect her.

He took a cab to the prison Eduardo was in. Everywhere he went in the foreign country he had to pay someone for information and their service. But he had a guide with him named Juan. For the right price, Juan was willing to help him. Still, Kamel knew he had to be careful. In New York, he was well known and respected, but in Colombia, he was a nobody at the bottom of the food chain. He stood out like a sore thumb. Everyone knew he was American, but Kamel held his head up and strode ahead.

He walked into the prison. He paid a few guards to lead him inside. He moved smartly, trying not to make himself into a victim. In Colombia, money does the talking.

The guards led him to a private room. He entered, and the door was shut behind him. He was alone and he was nervous. But he was ready to meet with Eduardo and say his piece. He stood and waited.

It was happening—it was happening now.

Kamel had no idea that Kola was in Colombia too. They'd both kept their motives a secret from one another. He had no idea that she was just in the same position that he was in about half-hour earlier. They'd barely missed each other.

The solid rusted door opened up, and a man stepped inside the room. Kamel looked at him. It was him, Eduardo, a huge looming figure. Even with Eduardo incarcerated Kamel felt intimidated.

They looked at each other intently.

Eduardo immediately knew the man was American.

"Eduardo?" Kamel asked nervously.

Eduardo's eyes narrowed. It didn't take a rocket scientist to know who the man standing in front of him was. He was surprised to see Kamel. He'd only heard about him, but he didn't expect to see the man in person. He didn't expect that he had the balls to travel so far to meet with him.

"I came to have a talk with you, man to man," Kamel said coolly.

"Man to man—and what kind of man are you?" Eduardo asked.

"I'm the kind of man that loves my woman greatly, and I will die for her if I have to. I respect you and your position, and came to ask for your permission," Kamel replied assertively. He didn't break eye contract with Eduardo but held his own inside the room.

"You have come a long way for such a foolish thing, Kamel."

"If I die, I die here, but I'm gonna die knowing that I tried everything to protect the woman I love."

Eduardo sat in one of the chairs, motioned to the other chair, and said, "Then have a seat, my friend, and let's talk man to man."

Kamel sat across from Eduardo. "Kola loves me, and I love her, Eduardo. I know everything about you because she speaks highly of you."

"I don't want to hear about her. I want to know about you."

"About me? What do you want to know?"

"Your history, your thoughts, your life and your family. Impress me somehow."

Kamel stared the man down. He took a deep breath and said, "I just murdered my twin brother. Shall I start there?"

Eduardo was intrigued by his statement. "Really?"

"Yes. He threatened Kola, your kids, and my well-being, so I put a bullet in the back of his head. That's the kind of man I am. I'll do whatever to protect what I love."

"So you're a twin?"

"Identical."

Eduardo nodded. He remained stoic and allowed him to continue talking.

Kamel went on to tell the kingpin about his history, where he came from, and what he had to do to reach the top. After talking about his street life, Kamel uttered, "I'm just tired. I just want a simple life, and I want to be normal. I want to open up my own business, maybe a body shop."

"Men like us, we can never be normal."

Kamel didn't believe it. He felt he could change his life and become someone different. Especially with Kola in his life.

"I love your kids like they're my own, Eduardo," Kamel said.

Hearing about his kids brought a touching feeling to Eduardo.

Surprisingly, Kamel had pictures of them, almost a dozen, of Sophia and Eduardo Jr. having a great time. He showed them to Eduardo. They were laughing and playing, and being part of a loving family. Kamel and Kola were in most of the pictures with the kids.

"They deserve happiness, Eduardo. They deserve better. Kola and I, we can give them that. Don't you want that for your children? I want to become a legit man for them. We both can't afford to have police kicking down my front door and risking their well-being. I understand your position, and I respect it. I'm not here to disrespect you, but I came here to plead for the lives of your children and their future. I love them too, and I will always protect them."

Eduardo was listening. Kamel had the gift of gab. What he was saying was tugging at Eduardo's heart. Eduardo could tell that Kamel was a man of honor.

"I'm willing to do right by you and your kids."

Eduardo didn't say a word. His look was intimidating, but Kamel didn't flinch. He sat across from one of the most powerful kingpins in the world and held his own, telling his story and not showing any weakness. If today was his day to die, then so be it. He felt good about himself. He saw something worth living for, or dying for—either way.

Eduardo still remained quiet, probably realizing that Kola and Kamel were the best shot at his children having a normal, happy life. He didn't want his kids pushed in harm's way. He wanted them to grow up without the sins of their father haunting their futures. Eduardo Jr. and Sophia could never be safe in Colombia. Also, he, Marisol, and Maribel were never going to get out of prison. Eduardo still had power and control, but he owed a political debt to his country, to significant people, and prison was his plea deal.

He removed a cell phone from his pocket and pushed a number. A call went through. Eduardo simply said into the phone, "Abort."

"¿Qué? the man replied. "¿Estás cierto?"

"Don't question me. I said abort!" Eduardo hung up.

He looked at Kamel and said to him, "You seem to be a man of your word, and I'll give you what you ask for, but a favor from me doesn't come free."

"I understand," Kamel replied.

"You are in debt to me, Kamel. And when I call in my debt, I expect you to pay," he said.

Kamel nodded.

He then said, "No body shop. They fail. You should open up a string of Chick-fil-A, or Subway restaurants. They will flourish. Let Kola help with running the books; she is good with numbers. She will work hard. And when my son is old enough you bring him in and show him the business. You do that for me, yes?"

Kamel nodded. "Yes."

"You will always allow Kola to take my calls and tell my children good things about their papa, yes? And when they are teenagers and they don't want to take my phone calls you nudge them to take my calls, yes?"

Kamel agreed.

After he was certain that Eduardo would allow him to live, Kamel had one more favor to ask of him. He needed help with taking care of Mack D. He explained the situation, and Eduardo listened intently. In the end, Eduardo promised that he would take care of it.

Kamel rode in the cab on his way from the jail. He was anxious. Eduardo had given him a location to go to, and he and Juan were hurrying there.

The minute he arrived at the site, he saw Kola alone and in tears. He was traumatized. Her captors had simply left her there after the phone call from Eduardo. Kamel hurried out of the cab and ran her way. He couldn't believe it. Kola was in Colombia, and she was almost killed. He ran to the love of his life and embraced her tightly. He didn't want to let her go.

They cried in each other's arms. It was time to leave Colombia and go home, but not before going for that buried treasure.

FORTY

Richard's death had Mack D so upset, he tore his office apart and smashed his flat-screens to the floor, cursing and insulting anyone in his way. He never thought Jamel would get the upper hand on his most lethal man. To add insult to injury, the girl murdered wasn't Apple, but the brothers' little sister. Who the fuck was Ana? However, it gave him some delight to know that the bitch was kin to the brothers.

Kola had lied to him. She had played him for a fool. He looked foolish—almost weak and incompetent—in front of his men. It seemed like the tide had turned on him.

Now Jamel was dead, but it wasn't by his soldiers' hands. Someone had gotten to him first.

Kola and Kamel were MIA. He assumed that they went underground, hit the mattresses, or left the city.

Mack D was determined to find them. He put such a high bounty on their heads, it was going to be impossible for them to run or hide anywhere, from state to state.

But then something or someone else grabbed his attention. It was an international call. The call he had been waiting for. He wasn't surprised that Eduardo had his cell phone number.

Mack D was excited that the kingpin himself had personally contacted him. He couldn't wait to do business with him. There were millions and millions of dollars to be made, if things went smoothly. Mack D planned on making sure every detail of the meeting with one of Eduardo's high-ranking lieutenants went as smoothly as possible.

"The bitch actually made it happen," Mack D said about Kola.

He believed that the pressure he had put on her finally made her buckle, and out of fear, she finally came to her senses.

The meeting was set up for the following evening at a warehouse near JFK Airport. He definitely wasn't going alone. He was going to bring an army with him. He didn't trust anyone, especially the Colombians.

The following evening, Mack D showed up at the airport warehouse in a caravan of SUVs. He came to the meeting deep with heavy artillery. Eduardo's men were already there, waiting for their arrival. Mack D smoked his cigar in the back seat and scanned the area. So far, everything looked copasetic. The doors to the warehouse opened, and they proceeded inside.

"Knowledge is power, but enthusiasm pulls the switch. So let's pull the switch on this fuckin' deal," Mack D said proudly.

Ten minutes later, the sound of heavy gunfire erupted, and it sounded like World War III had ensued.

Mack D had come with an army, but Eduardo's men had a bigger army and much heavier artillery. Twenty-one men, including Mack D, were never heard from again. No bodies were ever found. What the streets knew was that he was going to meet with the Colombians, and Eduardo was a ghost.

The streets, from Harlem to Brooklyn, were calm for a few months, and then all hell broke loose. As the cycle goes, a new reign of hard-core dealers came in and picked up where Mack D had left off.

EPILOGUE

Kamel and Kola stood on the Hawaiian beach holding hands and gazing at each other lovingly. The clean sand looked like sugar spread out for miles.

Kola looked beautiful in her long, white beach dress. She was glowing with happiness. Their marriage had been inevitable from the time they'd met. They were inseparable, and each was the center of the other's universe.

The pastor was ready to wed them. Peaches and Sophia were the flower girls, and Apple was the maid of honor. Eduardo Jr. was the ring bearer.

They spoke their vows to one another. Kamel was ready to live a different life and become someone new. As he stared at his beautiful bride, he thanked God for her. Today was the happiest day of his life.

They both said, "I do." They were now married.

Kamel was ready to kiss his bride. He moved his face closer to hers, and their lips met. When she kissed him, his brain lit on fire, and the warmth spread throughout his entire body. He was addicted to her. Her love and kisses were his salvation. She was the half that made him whole.

The children and Apple clapped. They all were excited.

Hawaii seemed like the perfect getaway. Their troubles felt like they were a lifetime away. Apple had her strong bond with her sister again, the children had a family; it felt like they had won. They'd prevailed against the odds.

But Kamel didn't forget about the unfinished business of the favor he owed Eduardo—what it took to keep them alive. Kamel was now in debt to the man, and Eduardo could call in the favor he owed any time.

From a distance away, three Colombian men clad in dark suits observed the happy couple. They simply watched, not interfering, but hovering over the newlyweds like a dark cloud. When the time came, Eduardo would come calling again, like a cancer out of remission.

For now, they all would live happily ever after.

Until their next chapter.

Don't Let the Dollface Fool You

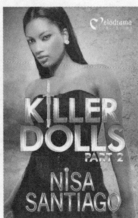

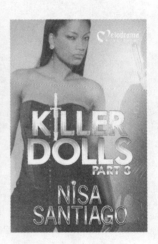

The new series By Nisa Santiago

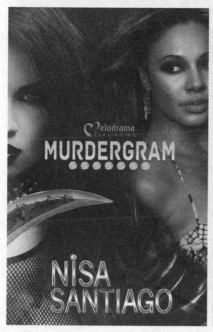

LET'S BUILD.

THE HOUSE THAT HUSTLE BUILT

NISA SANTIAGO

THE HOUSE THAT HUSTLE BUILT PART TWO

NISA SANTIAGO

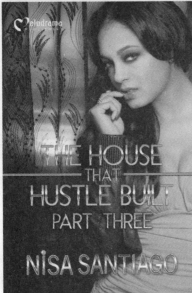

THE HOUSE THAT HUSTLE BUILT PART THREE

NISA SANTIAGO

A Series by
Nisa Santiago

All the Bad Girl
You Can Handle

Connect with us online at
MelodramaPublishing.com